ALISON BROWNSTONE

ALISON BROWNSTONE

THE UNBELIEVABLE MR. BROWNSTONE™ BOOK NINE

MICHAEL ANDERLE

THE ALISON BROWNSTONE TEAM

Special Thanks
to Mike Ross
for BBQ Consulting
Jessie Rae's BBQ - Las Vegas, NV

Thanks to the JIT Readers

Daniel Weigert
James Caplan
John Ashmore
Angel LaVey
Mary Morris
Peter Manis
Tim Bischoff
Paul Westman
Larry Omans

If I've missed anyone, please let me know!

Editor
Lynne Stiegler

To Family, Friends and
Those Who Love
to Read.
May We All Enjoy Grace
to Live the Life We Are
Called.

James stepped into the Black Sun, dried blood caked on his face and his current gray coat even shabbier than usual thanks to all the bullet holes. His shoulder and knee ached with each step, but it seemed like a waste of a healing potion for minor injuries.

That shit is expensive. I'm not a pussy. I can handle this.

Despite ambushing James, the bounty hadn't been the best shot in the world. He'd fought tougher opponents, but that didn't make the whole thing any less tiring or annoying.

The bounty hunter shook his head.

That's what I get for not using the amulet, but the fucker's gotten mouthier lately. I think I liked it better when I had no clue what the hell it was saying.

Now he just wanted a damned drink. Coming to the Black Sun hadn't been his first choice, but he'd already handed off the bounty to the police on the scene and he was close to the bar already, so it made more sense than driving all the way across town to the Leanan Sídhe.

A drink's a drink, right?

The few scattered thugs and miscreants sitting around the room spared the bounty hunter a quick glance when he came in before returning to their drinks and problems.

Since James hadn't kicked the door in or pulled a weapon, none of them had a reason to be afraid. James Brownstone wasn't anyone's idea of subtle, and everyone knew that. Rumors about him working with Tyler had also started getting out.

The bounty hunter grunted at the thought.

I wish Shay would stop calling us frenemies. I'm not a fucking teenage girl. I'm not planning to throw the asshole through a window, but that doesn't mean shit. We had an idea where we could both make money is all.

James dropped onto a barstool with a wince. He reconsidered the idea of using the potion but decided a beer would be enough to dull the pain.

Tyler finished polishing a glass and set it upside down on a rack. "Had a fun bounty, or is there some hit I need to start a betting pool on? Don't want to pass up a chance to make money off your ass." He grinned.

Are that asshole's teeth even whiter than the last time I saw them? Is that what he's spending all his money on now, tooth whitening?

James shook his head. "Sometimes fuckers think they'll get lucky, but their luck never lasts. I took the guy down already and gave him to the cops. No money to be made."

"Damn. Well, doesn't hurt to ask. You're like my own personal mutual fund."

The bounty hunter shrugged. "The guy wasn't a level

five. Not a huge amount of money for you even if you did get involved."

"Sometimes long shots make for more exciting and profitable betting." Tyler eyed Brownstone. "I wonder if we could work some sort of bounty-hunting equivalent of point shaving. Maybe you let the guy go at one fight, and then catch him later. If we set it up right, could make a lot of money off it."

James growled. "I'm not letting a bounty go when I catch him."

Tyler held up a hand. "Whatever. Was just tossing the idea out there. Calm down."

The bartender grabbed a bottle of Irish Stout for the bounty hunter and popped it using a bottle opener on the edge of the bar before handing it over. "Probably doesn't matter anyway."

"What do you mean?"

Tyler shrugged. "Yeah, I'm thinking the window for a lot of shit is closing with you. Hard to find people who still don't understand that you don't bet against Brownstone. Means there's a lot less profit potential for me." He sighed. "Still can make money off the streaming fees, though, if we ever decide to get another staged fight going. You know, a regular one where we get the guy to agree, and you pound him into dust. No letting him go."

"You still thinking about that? It didn't go so well last time."

The bartender leaned toward James and lowered his voice. "Look, we made good money off that, even with the problems. And you're still alive. So what's to complain about?" He shrugged. "Yes, we need to work out a few kinks, but I'm not convinced it was that bad of an idea. Great new ideas often take a little work to get going, especially ones involving a lot of money, and let me remind you that you remove some serious scum from the gene pool. Even if you don't give a shit about the money, that's got to make your bounty-hunting heart feel a little warmer."

James grunted. "My girlfriend is still busting my balls over the whole thing, talking about how I shouldn't have done it and all that shit. How it was dumb even though I won, but, yeah, I think you have a point." He shrugged. "What about Lieutenant Hall? Has she stopped kicking you in the balls yet?"

Tyler glanced around the room as if the AET lieutenant might jump from a darkened corner, railgun in hand, and blow his head clean off. Knowing the woman, James wouldn't doubt it.

"Nope." The bartender pulled a bottle of Jack Daniel's off the shelf and poured himself a drink. He took a sip before speaking again. "Just the other day, she told me how I'm a fucking moron and how she doesn't know if she did the right thing when she saved me from getting my ass kicked. Even said a few broken bones might have been a good lesson." He sipped more whiskey and let it burn down his throat. "I'm half-convinced she wanted me to end up in the hospital so she could gloat." He shook his head. "I don't even fucking get it. We set this shit up so no one would get hurt, including AET. We should be getting fucking medals, in my opinion. It was a good plan that just needed to be tweaked."

James nodded. "Yeah, I agree. I apologized and shit, but

the more I think about it, the less I understand why I was even saying sorry. Yeah, we didn't think about those fuckers pulling that gang-up bullshit, but next time—if there is a next time—we can figure out some shit, or I can just bring some back-up, too. Besides, they cheated, and *still* got their asses beat. It's the score at the end of the game that counts, not if the other team fouls you a few times."

"Exactly. I mean, if your woman's so worried about you fighting bad guys, she shouldn't let you go out and do bounties at all. Fuck, or destroy international criminal gangs. I'm sure fighting those assholes wasn't even in the top ten of dangerous shit you've done this year. Doing your job and getting extra money isn't stupid. It's fucking genius."

James nodded. "You're right."

Fuck, Shay helped me with the Harriken, but she's mad because I took on a few bounties without her. I respect her skills, but I was beating down level fives before I ever met her, and the amulet got stronger out of the whole thing. Now I know it can do stuff other than increasing my immunity and the telekinesis.

Shit, should really be practicing more with that thing, too. I've been afraid of it and not sure how to use it, but I keep running into people I can't just put down with a bullet. It didn't seem like I was being stupid.

Tyler gulped down more Jack. "And what's up with Maria being all pissy with me and acting like I've betrayed her trust or what the fuck ever? I've never hidden the kind of place the Black Sun is or the kind of man I am." He slapped a hand over his chest. "I seek out profit opportunities where I find them. I fucked over no one in this, including you, and I don't even like you. I did my best to help you, and even got the shit kicked out of me for it."

James grunted and let the other man continue his rant.

"For fuck's sake, one of the reasons I became friends with Maria was because of the betting shit I was doing on you before." Tyler pointed at his chest with a thumb. "And I'm never going to stop trying to make money, and it's not like I'm betting *against* your ass. I'm betting on your ass to beat down some bounties. How is it stupid to make money off something that's going to happen anyway? It's fucking common sense."

"It's not stupid." James finished his stout, and Tyler quickly supplied him with another one. "We did make money, and I'm not dead. Any fight you can walk away from is a win, no matter what the women are saying."

Two uniformed male police officers stepped into the bar. They did a quick survey of the patrons then headed toward a table, bored looks on their faces.

Tyler filled his own glass. "This isn't about your woman, or Maria, or even us. You know that, don't you, Brownstone? Don't let them fuck you over with their mind games."

"Huh? What do you mean?"

The bartender sipped some of his own drink and blew out a whiskey-soaked breath. "Men and women. Fuck. I think I get what's going on more in some male elf's head than a woman's, regardless of race. How messed up is that?"

James chuckled. "Yeah, I've been trying to listen to this podcast shit that explains it all, and it just makes me more confused. It's just not logical, and it's only talking about women."

"Exactly. They're accusing us of thinking with our dicks, but we weren't thinking with our dicks." Tyler tapped his forehead. "We were thinking with our fucking brain. Money. There were no emotions involved, and it wasn't about trying to impress people. And you were just trying to take down a fucker who you would have taken down anyway, all calculated using risk and reward."

"Yeah." The bounty hunter let out another small grunt and shook his head. "I got banged up, but there was no one else around. It's the safest fucking thing I've done in a while. Didn't have to worry about the highway getting blown up, or if there were innocent people who might get hurt. The guys involved didn't have some doom artifact that was gonna blow up the county." He frowned. "Fuck. You know the real bullshit in all this?"

"What?"

"My girlfriend does dangerous shit all the time and is constantly telling me she doesn't need me there, but I get yelled at for doing the same thing. How the fuck does that make sense?"

Tyler shook his head. "It makes not a single fucking bit of sense."

A huge, tattooed thug with a shaved head marched over to the bar, glass of vodka in hand. "I've got something to say, and you two fuckers are gonna listen."

James looked him up and down. The bounty hunter might still be sore from his earlier encounter, but he could boot the man across the room if necessary. He wasn't in the mood for any more bullshit, male or female.

Tyler gulped down the rest of his whiskey and slammed his glass on the counter. He narrowed his eyes at the thug. "And what the fuck do you have to say?"

"Bitches be crazy," the thug intoned. "Totally crazy. I've been with my woman for ten years now, and she's still busting my balls about shit she's known about forever. I'm like, 'Whatever, woman, you knew what I was when we got together, but now you're whining because I'm doing the same shit I've always been doing.' What the fuck is up with that? How is it fair?"

James chuckled.

Tyler slapped a hand down on the bar. "Exactly. Like I was telling Brownstone. This isn't about us. This is about the women. Why can't they just understand us? Are they even trying? We're trying to understand them. No damned reciprocity."

The thug nodded furiously. "Don't know what reciprocity means, but fuck yeah on the rest. Damn straight, brother. I'm not that hard to understand. It's not like I'm some fucking alien from another planet with pointy ears." He looked around for a moment, frowning, probably making sure there were no Oricerans in the room.

James grunted. Of course, the other men didn't know he was an alien, despite the lack of pointy ears, but that didn't change anything.

I believed in KISS. I made everything about my life simple. I still try to be simple. If Shay can't understand me, it's not my fault. She's making things complicated in her own head, and that's on her to fix.

Tyler grinned, his cheeks now flushed and his tongue loosened from his whiskey. "What about you, Brownstone?

What else have you done that your woman just doesn't understand?"

"My girlfriend complains because my house is clean and organized," James muttered. "What the fuck is wrong with that? Does she want it messy?"

The thug slapped him on the back. "I don't give a shit about keeping a clean place, but nothing wrong with you doing it. She's the crazy one, Brownstone, not you. Always remember that, brother."

Tyler laughed. "He's right. She shouldn't be trying to change you. Why isn't she just trying to understand who and what you are? Why is she insisting that you change? That's bullshit, I say. Bullshit." He stretched out the last word. "She's just being lazy and trying to make you feel guilty."

The thug gulped down some of his drink. "My woman comes to me a few weeks ago and complains about how this guy is talking shit to her and she thinks he needs to learn a lesson. So I go and pound his face, right? I didn't kill him or no shit. He can still even walk, but then she comes and bitches at me for 'taking things too far.' Motherfucker's still alive and walking. How did I take it too far? If anything, I didn't take that shit far enough."

Tyler chuckled.

James grunted. "Stupid podcast I listen to keeps saying that if a woman complains, she doesn't want you to fix something, and she might get mad if you do it anyway. Said it's presumptuous." He snorted. "How does it make any fucking sense not to go fix a problem that someone's complaining about? What's the point of talking about a problem you don't want solved?" He gestured around the bar. "I'm a bounty hunter. That's what I do. I fix problems."

"Nothing wrong with making problems go away," Tyler replied. "I think women should try to understand men as much as we try to understand them, even though you *can't* fucking understand them, ever."

The thug nodded his agreement.

It was about then the bounty hunter realized there were no waitresses present, and Kathy, Tyler's junior bartender and info broker, wasn't there either, let alone Lieutenant Hall. James couldn't help but wonder how much of Tyler's willingness to commiserate on the difficulties of women was based on the convenient absence of any females around him that evening.

Not that I'm much better. Shay isn't here. Or Alison. This damn amulet I've got under my shirt isn't bonded to me, and I doubt it's female. Then again, I can't understand what it's thinking most of the time and it likes to tell me what to do, so maybe it is.

James grunted, and the thug and Tyler both looked his way.

The two uniformed cops at the entrance of the Black Sun made their way toward the bar, one sitting on the barstool next to the thug, and another next to Brownstone.

The cop next to the thug, Ramirez according to his nametape, shook his head. "I've been married to my wife for five years. After our first date, she told me she only accepted because I was a cop, and she loves a man in uniform. So now what does she do all the time? Tells me I should stop being a cop because it's too dangerous, but I guarantee you if I quit the job to be some office drone, she'd be like, 'Why don't you have a job with more meaning?' You're not the same man I married."

The other men present all bobbed their heads in understanding.

Ramirez's partner Jackson snorted. "Yeah. Or how about this shit? My wife gives me a big speech about how society's too materialistic, and how the most important thing is just loving one another, and how we've lost all that in this country because we're slaves to the companies. She gives me this speech like a month before our anniversary." He shook his head. "So when our anniversary comes, she gets mad because I said we should just stay home and watch TV together, show our love, not waste money running around buying shit from companies, and she calls me a cheapskate." His eyes bugged out. "Now how is that fair? I think that's straight-up bullshit. I did exactly what she said she wanted, and I'm the bad guy."

"It's *not* fair, brother," the thug suggested. "It's so not fair. You listened, and she set you up, just like I was set up during my last arrest."

Ramirez nodded, as did Tyler.

James pushed his bottle away. "When I first met my girlfriend, she was upset about people not taking her seriously because of what she looks like."

"She super-hot?" Ramirez asked.

The bounty hunter nodded. "Yeah. Anyway, she got mad at me because I wasn't all over her." He shrugged. "I figured I was showing respect, but it pissed her off every time. She even kept saying I must be gay because I wasn't going after her. I kept telling her I wasn't gay, but she was acting like she didn't believe me."

Tyler refreshed everyone's drinks while they sat there pondering the mysteries of the fairer sex.

James waved off a new bottle. He would have to leave soon. The earlier beers had taken the edge off his injuries, so it was a good enough time to stop. Even though it took a lot for him to get drunk, no reason to take the risk with driving, especially given an important pick-up he had scheduled soon.

"What are we even supposed to do?" the bounty hunter asked. "If we ask what's up, half the time they say nothing, and they don't even try to understand why we're clueless. They just say shit about how we're thinking with our dicks."

The thug and cops laughed.

Tyler sipped more whiskey and nodded. "You're right, Brownstone. Respect and understanding should go both ways, but I feel like with our women, we have to do all the understanding of them, and they just get to yell at us."

I love her, but Shay doesn't understand me. That's for fucking sure. I don't mind, but I wish she wouldn't act like I'm a loser for not understanding her when she's all over the place.

James shrugged. "The real question is, what the fuck can we do about it?"

"Bitch about it at a bar, brother," the thug yelled. He raised his glass. "And drink our troubles away."

Tyler sighed. "We'll make them understand someday. Maybe some big Oriceran magic spell will be cast, and women will actually understand men instead of just assuming we're idiots, and men and women will never misunderstand each other again."

James doubted that even if he had a hundred wishes, he

could accomplish that. Some things were beyond the power of mere mortals.

"Sure. Miracles could happen, I guess."

Tyler shrugged. "We've got magic now, Brownstone. You know what I saw on the internet the other day?"

"A woman who actually understood her man?"

"Nope." The bartender shook his head. "A pig flying."

2

The target was close. Very close.

The woman watched from across the street as Alison stepped out of the train station, pulling a single pink rolling suitcase behind her. The teen had been gone for months, but she was comfortable returning home with only the smallest number of things.

Good, travel light, but you should be more aware of your surroundings. Bad people could be watching. Bad people like me.

The woman's lips curled into a smirk.

Alison pulled out her phone and held it for a moment, sighing. The woman didn't need magic to know what the girl was thinking.

This was the first time she'd traveled from the school by herself. It was obvious evidence of increasing ability with her energy sight, but that didn't mean traveling across the country was easy or comfortable. Being able to see energy wasn't the same thing as being able to see like an average person, and it had to make the experience awkward, at best.

Not only that, it made it a little dangerous. Just being able to see bad people wouldn't stop them.

Thinking about calling dear old Dad, huh, kid? Maybe you should before it's too late. But that's the thing. It already is.

The teen let out another long sigh and shook her head, a look of determination settling over her face.

Brave. Maybe not smart, but brave. You probably think you're big shit now because you've spent a year at the magic school. No, you're soft and used to being surrounded by a bunch of witches and wizards who keep the real monsters away.

Now, you're back in LA. Welcome to the land of monsters. You haven't noticed me yet because you weren't even trying to scan around.

The woman waited for the road to be clear and hurried across. She fell in behind Alison after the girl turned and headed down the sidewalk for a few yards.

The girl's energy sight might reveal the woman's presence if she turned around and knew what to look for, but fortunately, the large crowd entering and leaving the Starbucks would help hide her. There had to be more than a few dangerous people in the crowd with threatening-looking souls who would keep Alison's attention.

Can always depend on LA to deliver suspicious assholes when you need them.

Another teen girl emerged. She was laden with heavier suitcases, but she still rushed toward Alison, demonstrating surprising agility and strength as she pulled her stuff through the crowds on the sidewalk.

The woman narrowed her eyes. The new arrival was around Alison's age, but she didn't recognize the girl—although it wasn't like she'd memorized the face of every student attending the School of Necessary Magic. She had only one target, and that was Alison Brownstone.

Maybe she'd gotten bad information. The woman had been told the teen would be traveling alone, motivated by a desire to prove to her overbearing father that she didn't need to have her hand held.

Shit. Who the hell is this other girl? She might have some magic I don't know about. This could complicate things.

"Hey, Alison," the new girl called.

Alison turned around and smiled. "Hey, what are you doing here? I thought you were heading back to Alaska."

"Just visiting my aunt. It was kind of a spur-of-the-moment kind of thing." The girl shrugged. "We'll have to do something together, but I'm going to be in Mexico for the first half of the vacation. My aunt has a timeshare down there. Maybe when I get back?"

Alison smiled. "Oh, sounds cool. I'm sure we can figure something out."

"Yeah. What about you? Are you excited to be home? I mean, LA's a big city. Lots you can do here. We're not in the middle of nowhere like at school." The new girl laughed.

"Not sure." Alison sighed.

"Not sure if you're excited?" The girl frowned. "I don't get it."

"Yeah. Not sure."

"How can you not be sure?"

The woman following the teens slipped her hand into her jacket pocket. She was almost close enough to execute her plan. It was pretty much guaranteed to work now that

Alison was distracted. Too damned easy. The new arrival had been a blessing, not a threat.

A sense of satisfaction settled over the woman. Pulling off something like this in the middle of the night when everyone was sleeping would have been unimpressive, but accomplishing the task in broad daylight proved how clueless Alison Brownstone was.

The teen shrugged. "I'm excited, but I'm scared. I've been really yelling at my dad a lot recently when I talk to him on the phone, calling him stupid and stuff like that. I mean, he had it coming, because he was being totally dumb, but he probably isn't liking me too much right now."

The other girl gasped. "But…your dad is James Brownstone."

"Yeah, and?"

"You yell at James Brownstone? The Granite Ghost? The Scourge of Harriken? They said on the news the other day that he might be the single most well-known bounty hunter on Earth." The girl shrugged. "Probably Oriceran, too."

Alison rubbed her neck. "Granite Ghost? I forgot about that one." She laughed. "I mostly just call him Dad when I yell at him, but my mo…my aunt calls him a dumbass. Maybe we can call him the 'Granite Dumbass?'"

The other girl's eyes were saucers. "I still… Just, *woah*. I don't know. My dad's kind of stern, but he's not James Brownstone. I don't even know what I'd do if someone like Brownstone was my dad. I might be afraid to go home."

"Really?"

"Yeah, really."

Alison smiled softly. "He's not really like that, though. I

guess I'm maybe overreacting." She shrugged. "He's tough on bounties, but he's a good dad. Much better than my biological dad. I know that he loves me, but that doesn't mean he's not going to want to have a little talk when I get home. I can't help but be a little scared, even though I don't think I've done anything wrong."

An empty sedan pulled up to the curb with the Currus logo painted on the side. The woman following the girls didn't trust autonomous magical vehicles much, but at least there wasn't a driver to serve as an extra witness.

The teens' backs were turned. It was time. The woman moved to the side, so she was outside the angle of the car's forward cameras.

You should always be more careful, Alison. Never, ever assume that a crowd of people will protect you. Assumptions can get you killed within seconds.

The woman closed to within a few yards of the girls and grabbed a small warm capsule from her pocket. She glanced around, waiting a few seconds until no one was looking her way, then a quick flick of the wrist sent the capsule sailing toward Alison's suitcase.

It hit the back of the suitcase and melted silently in less than a second. A tiny, wriggling green beetle slipped in through a crack near the hinges.

Too fucking easy.

The woman smiled and stepped through the door into the Starbucks. She could use a drink. Her tracker was in place, and her job was done. She could go confront Alison Brownstone at her leisure.

It was an excellent test to see just how careful Alison and her father were.

You've got a lot of enemies, James Brownstone. You should never forget that, and you should never let your daughter forget it.

The Black Sun had filled up in the previous hour, though it maintained its standard sausage fest ratio of men to women. More and more men had overheard the conversation and joined the group at the bar, eager to share their befuddlement over women and confusion about how their significant others demonstrated a lack of understanding of men's behavior.

A waitress had come in for her shift, but she was eager to stay away from the main bar and all the bitching about how women didn't understand men.

As James pondered the various stories and anecdotes offered by his fellow men, a sudden realization struck him. He'd been so focused on Shay's anger that he'd forgotten that she wasn't the only woman in his life who'd had a few words to offer about his recent choices.

Damn. Really don't want things to be tense when I see Alison.

"Any of you have kids?" the bounty hunter asked.

Ramirez and Jackson shook their heads. Tyler looked disgusted by the idea. The other men around were split between shaking their heads and nodding.

The shaven-headed thug, who had introduced himself as Ralph only a few minutes before, nodded, then shook his head. At this point, he probably had more alcohol than blood in his veins, so his confusion wasn't surprising.

James chuckled at the man.

K2, another bounty hunter, sighed. "I have kids. Two sons. Fucking teenagers. Old enough to be pains in the ass, but not old enough to give me rent money. Think they are big shit, though." He snorted. "What's up with them trying to smart off? I bring in bounties for a living. I'm not afraid of two punk-ass kids."

"At least they're sons, so they understand you, and you understand them," James grumbled. "It would be a lot more confusing if they were daughters. More women to not understand you."

"Huh? You got a kid, Brownstone? I didn't even know that." K2 chuckled. "Kind of funny to think of an ass-kicker like you as a dad. Guess you'll have the toughest son in LA."

James shrugged. "Working on finalizing an adoption, but not a son. A daughter. A teen."

Several of the men winced.

"Yeah." The bounty hunter nodded. "I don't understand half the shit going on with her. Cries when she's mad. Cries when she's happy. Wants me to kick ass some days, but wants me to hide and switch jobs on others. To be fair, though, she's had a tough life. Maybe that's why she's like that."

K2 laughed. "Doesn't matter if she had the most normal life in a boring suburb. I would never even try and understand a teenage girl. Might as well ask me to reveal the secret of life." He put a hand on James' shoulder. "I feel your pain, Brownstone. You seem like a straight-forward guy, or at least that's the way you've always come off here or when you're blowing up Harriken buildings."

Everyone laughed, but James only offered another grunt.

"The point is," K2 continued, "guys like us like to keep things simple, right?" He dropped his hand.

"Yeah, exactly. That's how I've tried to live my life. Keep it simple, stupid. And I used to be able to until I got involved with all these women."

"Keeping things simple is not just about being straightforward." K2 slammed his fist into his palm. "And when it comes to bounty hunting, that means kicking ass first and asking questions later. That shit doesn't always work with parenting or women, so parenting a soon-to-be woman's got to be tough, especially when your woman is giving you shit and being confusing. You've got it real bad."

James glanced down at his phone. He'd been expecting a message from Heather, but the hacker hadn't so much as sent him an emoji. Given the nature of her current task, he doubted she was in personal danger, which meant there'd been no movement of the target yet.

Maybe I got the schedule wrong. Probably should at least clean up a bit before I go face my next serious opponent of the day.

Tyler rubbed his chin. "Don't you see what's going on here, gentlemen? Don't you see the truth staring us in our faces?" He shook his head. The whiskey had reddened his face.

Everyone looked his way.

The bartender gestured grandly. "We've got cops here, robbers—"

Ralph shook his head. "I'm no robber. I kick ass, but I don't usually take people's shit. Guess that makes me, what? An assaulter?"

Tyler gestured toward a few other criminals. "Semantics. Plenty of other robbers here."

A couple of other thugs shrugged and grinned.

"Just saying," Ralph muttered.

Tyler rolled his eyes. "Anyway, as I was saying, we've got cops, assaulters, robbers, bounty hunter, and bartenders. The point is, we're all different men with different career paths, and we're even on different sides of the law. We're all interested in and deal with different kinds of women of different backgrounds, and yet we all have the same fucking problem. Do you know what that problem is?"

No one said anything as they stared at Tyler.

"We're all fucking clueless about women." Tyler shook a finger. "We've been brought together today by the fact that no matter what we do and how hard we try, our women keep surprising us and making us question the very reality we see before us. Think about that shit, gentlemen. It's fucked up. It's almost magic-level fucked up."

The motley gathering all nodded and grumbled their agreement. A few people even offered a, "Hell yeah, it's fucked up."

James turned away and let a little smile play on his face. He hadn't been sure about stopping by the Black Sun earlier, but now he was glad he had. For once in his life, he didn't feel like such a freak. He'd never been good with people, let alone women, and after finding out he was an alien, he'd assumed that was the reason.

How could a man born on another world ever hope to understand humanity? That was what he'd wondered. The average Oriceran might be an alien in a sense, but the long-standing ties between their world and Earth made the situation seem different, unlike James and his mysterious amulet.

But now he was sitting in a bar where half the men admitted to being just as clueless as he was when it came to women. It proved that James wasn't a freak, or at least not any more of one than a man born on Earth, and that his inability to understand Alison and Shay was more about them being more complicated than him being a dumbass.

See, Shay? See?

Heather hadn't confused him too much yet, but he assumed it was just a matter of time.

As if the woman had hacked into his thoughts, his phone chimed with a text from her.

The target is getting close to the rendezvous point. You should probably get going.

James slipped the phone back into his pocket, stood, and reached inside his jacket. Everyone tensed, their eyes locked on him, expecting a knife, grenade, or his now famous .45. There were more than a few men at the bar with bounties, and no one was sure how much the bounty hunter respected the neutrality of the Black Sun, even if he had stopped by to drink a pint or two.

No weapon came out, only a wallet. James tossed several large bills on the counter with a grunt.

Tyler eyed the money. "Leaving?"

"Yeah, and I want to make sure the cops are taken care of, but there's more than enough to take care of everyone else in this conversation," James rumbled.

Tyler eyed the bounty hunter, suspicion playing in his eyes. "That's unusually generous of you. Not saying you're a count-the-pennies kind of guy, but I have never heard about you buying rounds for people."

"What can I say? Got to support my fellow confused brothers. I learned today that we all have a lot more in common than I thought."

The bartender chuckled. "Keep doing shit like this and someday I might actually like you, Brownstone."

"It's like you said, Tyler, these days, pigs fly."

Tyler smirked. "So why you leaving? Bounty?"

"Just someone I need to meet. They've made some mistakes recently, said some shit I'm sure they regret, but I'm hoping that won't be a problem when it comes to LA." James gave the gathered men a polite nod and marched toward the front door.

Hope this shit doesn't blow up in my face.

3

James took a deep breath as he sat behind the wheel of his F-350 in the parking lot of an Arby's. His hands tightened around the wheel, and his stomach refused to unknot. He hadn't been this nervous in years. Then again, this wasn't the kind of encounter he had a lot of experience with.

Fuck. Need to calm down. Not like I need to crack out the amulet for this shit. Just need to learn how to handle it, and the only way I'm gonna do that is directly and through practice.

He grunted. Much had happened, but he had so much still to learn.

Cool metal pressed against his chest, the metal separator that prevented the amulet from bonding with him. He still hadn't gotten that used to taking the amulet with him everywhere he went, but considering who he was about to meet, there was no way he couldn't wear it. The risk of discovery was just too high, especially after he'd promised he would.

A Currus car pulled into the parking lot and pulled to a stop. A moment later, Alison exited with her suitcase and a smile on her face.

Time to see how everything's gonna go. She's been so pissed with me lately, and I don't want to start off summer vacation with another fight. She looks happy though.

James hopped out of his truck and headed her way. The Currus sped away from the parking lot guided by its inscrutable combination of magic and technology, leaving the bounty hunter to face his greatest opponent in weeks—his teenage daughter.

The bounty hunter blew out a breath and stopped in front of the girl, wondering what he should say, or if he should even be the first one to talk. They'd talked since her last major rage attack, but she'd made it very clear she wasn't happy with James' foray into bounty hunting pay-per-view, and she'd declared some of his other decisions "boneheaded and stupid."

I stand by what I did. If she wants to talk about it, we can discuss how things didn't go the way I planned, but I'm not gonna act like it was the dumbest thing I've ever done. I'm the adult here, and I'm the professional bounty hunter.

Alison stood in the parking lot for a few seconds before letting go of her suitcase and rushing over to James. She wrapped her thin arms around him in a loving hug.

Relief spread through the bounty hunter. He'd half-expected her to channel her inner Shay and curse him out first thing. He could understand her frustration, but she also needed to understand who he was and what he did. It wasn't like he was going to suddenly stop being a bounty hunter because he had a girlfriend and a kid. If anything, he needed to be stronger to make sure he could protect the people he cared about.

"I'm so glad to be home," Alison murmured into his chest, her arms still around him. "I know we've seen each other on parents' weekends, but it's been too long since we could really just sit and relax, you know?"

James smiled and patted her head. "I'm glad you're home too, kid. I know that school is good for you, but that doesn't mean I don't miss you every day you're gone."

Alison pulled away and grabbed her suitcase. "Are you mad that I made you pick me up here? I know it's kind of a weird thing, but I just want you to get used to me being a little more independent, and I thought this was a good way to do it halfway without giving you a complete heart attack."

He shrugged. "I get that you're getting older, and you've been going to a fancy magic school, and all that shi—stuff. I also get that you want your independence, but I don't see why you couldn't just have taken the car right to the house. I mean you came across the country by yourself, so why make me come and get you here?"

James glanced at the restaurant. A few people had their phones out and were taking pictures of him through the window—the annoying price of fame.

"Maybe I wanted you a little uncomfortable to drive the point home." The teen grinned. "Plus, I thought I'd want some roast beef, but now suddenly I don't." She laughed. "I'm a little hungry, but I can wait."

They made their way to the F-350. James hurried to the

passenger side to open the front and back doors. He grabbed Alison's suitcase and tossed it in the back seat before closing the back door, extending his hand to help the girl into the front.

Alison waved him off. "I remember the truck, and things aren't the same as the last time I was in LA."

"You're still blind."

"But my energy sight's improved a lot. You've seen me at school. More magic has made things easier for me." She shrugged. "You're just going to have to get used to that."

James grunted. "That school is different than LA. It's filled with a bunch of people who want to help you. This is a city, where people are assholes and don't want to help anyone. They don't care about anyone but themselves."

Alison laughed. "You're more dramatic than some of the theater kids I know." She hopped into the truck without any hesitation or difficulty and closed the door. "See? I'm fine. No big deal."

James circled around the other side and stepped up to his seat. "Just saying, things aren't always safe. Keep that in mind." He glanced at her. "Do you still have your Aegis Pendant?"

He sucked in a breath. It wouldn't be easy to replace the artifact, but he'd do what he needed to protect Alison.

The teen pulled the pendant out from under her shirt. "Yes, I do, but I'm not the person who is doing dangerous bounties or getting jumped by Drow thugs. You made a promise to me, so the real question is, do you have your amulet?"

The bounty hunter retrieved the inactive artifact from under his shirt. "Yeah, I do. I'm slow sometimes, but not stupid." He started the car and pulled out of the parking lot. "And I always keep my promises."

James had thought about messing with Alison and claiming he didn't have the amulet, but the girl could detect lies. That made the whole thing pointless.

She might be able to detect lies, but she still can't read my thoughts. Thank God for that. I'm not completely outmatched yet.

A small dagger of guilt stabbed James. Alison knew about the amulet, but she didn't know everything about it, including its alien origin or even the fact that it seemed to be intelligent. Fortunately, she also hadn't asked. He, on the other hand, knew everything about her half-Drow heritage and even controlled her wish.

It's for her own good. She already worries way too fucking much about me. The last thing I need to do is saddle her with more of my weird-ass baggage.

I'm the adult here, and she's the kid who's had to deal with losing her mom and a sonofabitch father who sold out her mom to the Harriken and was even willing to send Alison to them.

James shook his head. That was the past. He needed to focus on having a good time with her this summer. "How was your ride?"

Alison shrugged. "Oh, it was fine. I spent less time on that train than you spent coming to pick me up." She smiled.

"And you didn't have any trouble? You don't always tell people you're blind, even when you should." James frowned and imagined going to the train station and having a couple of intense conversations with assholes who messed with his daughter.

Alison laughed. "It wasn't that hard. Just took the bus from the school. Everyone was fine and nice. It's not like Virginia is some warzone crawling with bounties and Drow assassins, Dad." She rolled her eyes. "Apparently unlike LA."

James shook his head. "I just don't know if it was a good idea to let you travel by yourself, even with you being better at magic. What if the Drow come after you when I'm not around, or you're not at the school?"

"You kicked their asses, and I doubt they're coming back anytime soon. We can just relax and have a good summer, you know? I know you're not going to take off work the entire time, but I'm hoping we still can do a lot together."

He spared her a glance accompanied by a faint smile. "Oh, don't worry. I'm gonna make sure we spend all sorts of time together. We've got months to spend together, and I want to make sure it's all memorable."

Alison beamed. "Good."

"Well, you said you're not hungry for roast beef, but what about food in an hour? Shay said she'd be landing soon and coming in an hour. We could go get some pizza then."

"Not barbeque?" Alison turned to look at him as if confirming he was telling the truth.

"This is about you, not me." James shrugged. "Shay's coming back and I figured pizza would work for her, but we can do barbeque if you want."

Alison laughed. "I like barbeque, but not as much as you. Let's do pizza."

Yev took several breaths. Being consul in Los Angeles had always been a stressful position, but in recent months, the damned Drow had pushed him to his absolute limit. He'd thought they were done with their idiotic and blunt machinations, but the imminent arrival of one of the king's personal advisors suggested that something more serious and painful was coming the consul's way.

Damned Drow. You should have just left well enough alone. Now you've complicated things for us in this city. Are you trying to start a war? You're worse than Rhazdon, in a way.

Faint music drifted in the air. The portal was coming.

A bright line sliced through the air in front of his desk and a portal spread out from the line, an ornate council chamber from the king's castle on the other side. The Light Elf official stepped through the gateway to Earth with a pinched expression on his face as if he were in the last place he wanted to be.

The official sighed. "It feels different even just standing here on Earth. I should have known. I can only imagine getting used to the smell."

The beauty of the elegant, musical Light Elf language was not lost on Yev. Even though he was far from the only Light Elf in the consulate, he spent far too much of his day not speaking his own language, especially with all the forced interactions with humans of late.

Yev stood out of respect. "And this is the first time you've visited Earth?"

"Yes. I've seen little reason to." The official sat in the chair in front of Yev's desk. "The necessity of what might come in the future isn't the same as the necessity of now. I suppose those like you will have an advantage."

The consul nodded and sat. "This planet has its charms. I don't know if you'd find most of them in this city, though. It's a chaotic and often dangerous place. Humans have handled the return of magic...poorly in many cases, and LA continues to prove that each day."

"I can imagine." The other elf smirked. "Before we continue, I want to say that you've done well. Let me make that clear.

"Thank you."

The official nodded. "You're welcome. The king understands your efforts, as does everyone of importance. The plans of the Drow will likely continue, but for now, the damage has been contained to their reputation and the loss of their people, and our attention on them in Oriceran should keep significant trouble from spilling over to Earth for some time."

"I'm relieved to hear that," Yev offered. "I was beginning to think the next Great War would be fought with LA as the first major battleground."

"Even the Drow queen understands the delicate situation here." The official sighed and shook his head. "Which is why it's so frustrating that we're still forced to aid them, even if indirectly."

Yev frowned. "Excuse me? Why would we aid the Drow after everything they've done?"

"You are aware that this James Brownstone intends to adopt the girl that the Drow had such interest in, and that she is half-Drow, correct?"

"Yes. I previously encouraged them to handle this situation in a more diplomatic manner, but their arrogance sent them down a different path." Yev's lip curled into a sneer. "They are the ones who saw fit to send assassins and teams of warriors. They are the fools who attacked the local human anti-magic authorities. We're just fortunate they didn't kill any of them. I don't think those of you who spend time on Oriceran can appreciate how savage and given to vengeance Earth humans can be." He sighed. "The Drow could have destroyed years of outreach efforts."

The official gave Yev a tight look that suggested he was more annoyed than concerned. "I understand that, but this isn't about the Drow. Or at least, they aren't the problem we need to solve. It's Brownstone and the girl, Alison."

Yev shrugged. "What do we care? Isn't the adoption a good thing?"

"Oh? You think it's a *good* thing?" The official arched a brow. "Explain."

"The girl can serve as the perfect symbol of the new relationship between Earth and Oriceran, given that she is a true child of both worlds." Yev smiled. "I'm very familiar with the human media landscape. We should be talking to Brownstone about setting up interviews. Maybe even offer the girl some time on Oriceran to appreciate her heritage. We can keep her away from the Drow if we feel that's necessary."

The official shook his head. "If only it were so simple. No. She's half-Drow, and not just any half-Drow, after all, but the current Princess of the Shadow Forged. The Drow might have ceased their attacks for now, but they've made it clear they will not tolerate her becoming part of Brownstone's family, and given her royal status, it's difficult for us to simply ignore them or deny them some input in this matter."

"Meaning what?"

The official folded his hands and sat back. "If this adoption goes through I suspect there will be war, so we have to push back against this. We need to make sure Alison stays independent of James Brownstone. This adoption cannot proceed."

Yev sucked in a breath. "We can't."

"We must."

"You don't understand." The consul shook his head. "If we establish a firm line of separation between Oriceran and Earth and suggest we won't support adoption of Oricerans, half-blooded or otherwise, we're setting a dangerous precedent." He grimaced. "You don't understand the strength of some of the anti-Oriceran groups here. This could undo years of diplomatic work, and help persuade the humans that what Oriceran intends isn't harmony but invasion. I'm sure the other consuls and ambassadors would offer similar thoughts on the matter."

The official frowned. "Then we need another alternative. No matter what, James Brownstone can't be allowed to adopt that girl. You're one of our most experienced on this planet. What do you suggest?"

"I'll only note that if you intend to confront him directly, even in a less-violent manner, it's ill-advised given what's happened with the Drow. We have to do this in a way he can't or won't resist. I will also say that James Brownstone has great respect for the local human authorities. That's something we could use against him."

"Yes." The official gave Yev a dark grin. "You're right. We will do this through their system."

"Their system?"

The official nodded. "We shall use their courts to make it clear that it's okay for a human to adopt an Oriceran, but not okay for James Brownstone to adopt that *particular* Oriceran."

4

J ames finished gobbling down his fourth slice of pepperoni pizza and set his plate back on the dining room table. Shay had texted to him to say she'd be a little late, so he went ahead and grabbed the pizza. Alison and the bounty hunter had attacked it as they waited for the third part of their strange family—everyone's favorite aunt-slash-tomb raider—to arrive.

Wonder why she's late? Some sort of last-minute tomb raid? Hope she isn't too pissed that we started without her, but we can always go get more pizza or have some delivered.

Or maybe not. James frowned. There were very few delivery pizza places Shay could tolerate. For a woman who used to be a professional killer and often crawled around in the dirt and the mud, she could be rather fussy and particular.

James grunted. Somehow when he obsessed over something he was OCD, but for her, it was just common sense or good taste.

Tyler's right. I don't think I'll ever understand women.

Alison finished her single slice of pizza. "Guess I'm still not that hungry. The pizza *is* a lot better in LA, though." She laughed. "Not that the food at the school is bad. Just different, and everything here is very familiar in a way the school isn't at times." She shrugged.

"That's the big city for you. Lots of different nice places to eat." James smiled. "Plus, pizza's got a lot of protein." He eyed her. "Protein's good for building muscle. You could use a little more muscle."

"Not like I'm going to be a bounty hunter. I don't need to be as buff as you, Dad."

The front door beeped, then opened, which meant someone with access to the security system was coming in. No tension assailed the bounty hunter since he'd been expecting Shay, though he was a bit surprised she'd not bothered to text him before her arrival.

Hope this is a good sign.

James turned toward the door. Shay stepped inside with a scowl on her face.

Shit. Guess whatever was going on with her job left her in a bad mood. Sucks that it had to be on Alison's first day back. Hope she doesn't make it a big deal. Want everything to be nice and relaxed.

The tomb raider's gaze landed on Alison, and a smile wiped the scowl off her face. She headed over to give James, then Alison, a hug.

"Glad to have you back in LA, Alison."

The girl beamed a bright smile at Shay. "I'm so glad to be back, Aunt Shay." She pointed to the pizza box on the dining room table. "Thin crust, your favorite."

"Good, but you have to understand that it's not that it's my favorite."

James blinked. "Since when?"

"You don't get it. This is less about my tastes and more that it's the only kind of real pizza." Shay's scowl returned, and she stepped away from Alison. The tomb raider crossed her arms. "But before I get into the pizza, I've got a little confession for both of you."

Alison and James exchanged glances.

"I didn't fly into town just now," Shay continued. "I've actually been here since this morning, working on a little personal job that had nothing to do with tomb raiding."

James shrugged. "It's not a big deal if you had stuff to take care of. We understand. At least you weren't off in the middle of the desert or something. Could have given me a call, though."

Alison nodded. "Anything cool that you can tell us about?"

Shay smirked. "Yeah. I can tell you all about the job because it involved you."

"Me?"

James frowned. "What the hell are you talking about it? Is someone targeting Alison?"

Shay ignored him, shook her head, and pointed to Alison's suitcase. "When you're at that school, I don't worry. They are up to their asses in witches, wizards, and weird magical monsters. It's probably why the Drow never went after you directly. Too much magical defense, and that is if they could even detect you, to begin with. I'm guessing the fact they kept causing trouble in LA meant that they couldn't."

Alison shrugged. "The school does have powerful magic around it. Not like that's a secret. What's the big deal? Isn't that a good thing?"

Shay looked between James and Alison, frowning. "Seriously? Neither of you?"

"Seriously what?" Alison asked.

James shrugged.

The tomb raider closed her eyes and took a deep breath. She opened her eyes, and a mask of disappointment descended over her face. "The girl's one thing, but you, too, James? I guess that's the real disappointment."

He grunted. "What the hell are you talking about? What is this job? Who hired you?"

Shay crossed her arms. "I was thinking maybe I shouldn't do anything until you two figure it out, but I'm hungry, so I guess I better hurry this along. No one hired me. I hired myself."

She marched over to the suitcase and unzipped it. The tomb raider reached inside and pulled out a tiny green beetle. She held it up and shook her head. "Get it now?"

James frowned but didn't say anything, not understanding the implications of some strange green beetle in Alison's luggage. Maybe the School of Necessary Magic had a pest problem, or the beetle was some strange Oriceran creature that liked to wear unnecessary top hats.

Alison tilted her head. "It's magical, but it's like the magical aura has been suppressed somehow. If I'm not looking right at it, I can barely even see it."

Shay rubbed the back of the beetle. It glowed for a few seconds, and a green shell formed around the bug. She stuck the now-formed capsule in her pocket and sighed.

"Do you have any idea what that was, kid?"

Alison shrugged. "A bug?"

The tomb raider nodded. "Yes, in many senses of the word. It's a tracking bug. It's very easy to track from a long distance with very little effort. Of course, one major disadvantage is that you have to get close enough to plant the damned thing, to begin with."

Alison blinked. "Wait. You planted a magical tracking bug on me?"

"You're damned right I did."

"But why? You could have just called me if you wanted to know where I was."

Shay shook her head. "You made such a big deal about independence and proving yourself that I decided to do a little test. I flew into town before you got here and followed you at the train station. I planted the bug to see if you'd figure it out." She frowned. "I was basically right behind you and your friend when I did it, but you never even noticed me."

James frowned. "Friend? What friend? What was his name?"

Alison rolled her eyes. "It was a girl, Dad. Calm down."

"Oh." The bounty hunter nodded, satisfied. "No big deal."

Shay patted her pocket. "Wrong. This *is* a big deal because of the other big disadvantage of the bug. You can crush it just like any other bug or throw it out, so if you'd found it, it would have been very easy to handle, but you *didn't* find it. You had no idea it was there. So not only could someone have tracked you, but they could have tracked you all the way to your home and taken you out when they felt like it.

Alison sighed. "Um, sorry?"

The tomb raider shook her head. "Not good enough. Not damned good enough. That school might be teaching you magic, but that doesn't change the fact that people are targeting you—dangerous people—and once you leave that school, you're at risk. You have to get your head in the game, kid, or the next thing you know you'll be in some Drow dungeon crying." She pointed at James. "No matter how tough he is, he won't be able to do crap for you if you're on Oriceran. The people sniffing around for you have major magic. It was too close the last time the Drow came knocking."

Alison looked down at the floor.

James frowned. "Come on, Shay. It's not that she shouldn't be a little more careful, but you don't have to be such a bi… You don't have to be so harsh about it."

The tomb raider spun toward James and shook a finger at him. "*Harsh?* You're not off the hook either there, daddy dearest. I've got major harshness to still drop."

"Huh?"

Shay sneered. "Remind me again what the Drow have been doing here on Earth? Because from what I can tell, it's mostly been them trying to kill you. You might have forgotten that with all your dumb stunts with that idiot from the Black Sun, but don't think I have."

Damn it, when is she going to stop complaining about that?

James grunted. "It doesn't matter. I'm still alive. They aren't, and from what the cops told me, according to the consulate, there won't be any more Drow coming for a while. We won, and the Oricerans are gonna keep an eye on them."

"Oh, that's what you're depending on? Oricerans guaranteeing they've got those rule-breaking assholes already under control?" Shay marched over to the bounty hunter, her eyes narrowed and her hands on her hips. "If you don't make sure she is clean, you'll be having to dig Drow out of your ass, and even with the amulet it won't be enough."

Alison sighed. "I'm sorry. I should have been more careful. You're right, Aunt Shay. With my sight, I should be checking everything and everyone more often. If I had been paying more attention, I would have found the bug."

James glanced at the girl and back to Shay. He didn't want to undermine the importance of security, but he also didn't like the idea of the girl being depressed about failing some insane Shay test involving magic bugs on her first day back. They'd gotten through all the tension from the last few weeks, and there was no reason to bring it back up.

"We get the da… We get the point," James rumbled. "Going on and on about it won't help anything now." He shrugged. "Why don't you just eat some pizza and calm down?"

Shay rubbed her temples, stepped back, and took a deep breath. "You're right, and I'm hungry. Haven't had anything but coffee for a while." She headed over to the dining room table to grab a slice. "You do get, Alison, that I'm not riding you for no reason? I'm not just trying to be a bitch here. I worry about you, and I want to do everything I can to make your life safer."

The girl nodded. "I know you care, Aunt Shay, and I'll

try to do better in the future. It's not like…" She shrugged. "Learning magic isn't like learning stuff in a normal classroom. It keeps me more on my toes than you think, and my abilities *have* improved."

"Good. I just really think it'd be annoying if James and I have to go invade Oriceran to get you back." Shay offered Alison a grin. "Even though it'd be fun to see him destroy an entire world."

Alison chuckled and smiled back.

James shook his head. "I don't even like going down to Mexico. But it doesn't matter. We'll be going on vacation there soon enough, but for this week, I've got a few things to take care of." He looked at Alison. "I want you to come along so we can spend more time together."

The teen nodded. "Sounds good, Dad."

Shay bit into her pizza and smiled. "This is actually pretty good." She winked at James. "You've finally bought a clue about true pizza."

Yev leaned back in his chair, the phone to his ear. "I understand how this might cause some issues, Senator, but as I've explained, this adoption can't proceed, not with that man and that girl. The level of political fallout for both worlds is just too high. It could unravel everything we've both worked for these last few years. You've been a great benefit to the consulate in the past, and we only hope you'll continue to realize the importance of what we do here."

The senator sighed on the other end. "I want to be angry and scream at you about America being the land of second chances, but I appreciate how you've always been straight with me in the past about bullshit that might harm California or the country. I don't know how the other consuls and ambassadors handle things, but you're a good egg, Yev, and I'm glad I've been dealing with you."

Good egg? The Light Elf frowned. After all these years on Earth and in the United States, he still had trouble understanding their mindset and idioms at times.

"I appreciate your understanding, Senator, but we'll need a little more direct assistance in defusing this matter."

"What do you mean?"

Yev sighed. "If Oricerans openly oppose the adoption, we risk empowering anti-Oriceran groups. We're all too aware of the people just waiting for an appropriate rallying cry to convince people of alleged nefarious deeds. Blocking the adoption of a photogenic teenager by the world's most famous bounty hunter would risk political damage that might take us years, if not decades, to recover from. We can't be seen as having a direct hand in this. I'm all too aware of how manipulative many people feel Oricerans are, and elves in particular."

"I get that, so what are you suggesting, then? Obviously something more than just asking him not to do it."

"You're, of course, much more familiar with your laws and culture. What I'm about to pass on to you comes directly from a king's advisor—and thus the king, just to make that clear." Yev took a deep breath. "We'd ask that your government play the role of the reluctant party. That you find some sort of reason based on Earth laws and customs to oppose the adoption, preferably something specific to Brownstone."

The senator clucked his tongue. "This won't be one of the things I've done in my career that will make me proud later, but I'll call around and pull some strings. I'm sure someone at a lower level can figure out a plausible-sounding excuse to stop this. That is, if you're sure there's no other way?"

"Unfortunately, Senator, I'm very sure. We must do whatever it takes to make sure James Brownstone doesn't adopt the girl, for the good of Earth and Oriceran."

5

Manuel gesticulated wildly as he finished telling his story. "So I told the motherfucker, 'If you're the twin, then you won't mind coming with me to the police station, right?' Then the fucker tries to stab me, so I knocked his ass clean out. Stupid-ass bounties. Why do they always try that shit?"

The gathered men laughed. They were about half the total strength of the agency. The other men were out on jobs, including the current Vegas team.

Shorty grinned. "Man, you should have heard some of the shit Trey was telling me about." He looked around. "Where is he, anyway? I ain't seen him all day."

"Working a job," Manuel replied.

"I thought he was training with us today."

"He… What the fuck?" Manuel's attention slid past Shorty, and the men gathered by the pit followed his eyes to James, who was marching out of the Brownstone Building with a hot thin girl wearing track shorts, a t-shirt, and tennis shoes. Her pale skin contrasted with her dark hair, except for the white on the ends.

James gestured around the area. "This is the main training area. It's for body weight exercises. You'll do runs, too, but not without me or some of the men, Alison."

Alison shook her head. "Are you serious? This is how you want to spend time together? Making me exercise? That doesn't sound like a lot of fun."

The bounty hunter grunted. "You're not exactly in Shay shape."

"But we had PE in school," the girl whined. "I'm not going to be a bounty hunter. I don't need to be in that good of shape. Not Shay shape or James Brownstone shape."

He shrugged. "No one said you had to be as good as us, but endurance can save your life. Shay's right. We were both sloppy, and I was already planning a lot of this anyway. Just going to do more of it right away."

Shorty and Manuel exchanged glances. Max stepped toward the men.

"Is she a new trainee?" Max adjusted his glasses and lowered his voice so only the other bounty hunters could hear him. "Damn, she's hot. But why would Brownstone bring in a chick like that? Is she gonna work with Charlyce?" He furrowed his brow. "Wait, can we date co-workers?"

Shorty frowned. "What the fuck you talking about?"

"I don't remember signing shit about not dating anyone at work. That's not against the rules, right? She don't look like she's gonna be working jobs, so it's not like it'd mess anything up when we're out tracking bounties." Manuel shrugged.

Shorty laughed. "You serious, man? She's hot, but I think she's a don't-you-dare-touch-me kind of girl. She's probably some girl Brownstone saved from a fucked-up serial killer, and now he's trying to train her so she can kick ass as part of her therapy or some shit. Because that's the way Brownstone rolls. He makes people fucking better than they were."

"I don't remember him saying shit about bringing anybody," Manuel replied.

Daryl, who had been stretching nearby, laughed. "Y'all a bunch of dumb motherfuckers. Don't you know shit about anything?"

The men all turned to him, most looking even more confused than before.

Shorty snorted. "What are you talking about, you loud-mouthed fool?"

Daryl nodded toward the girl. "That's Alison, you dumb shit. As in Alison Brownstone, the girl he's adopting. That's James Brownstone's motherfucking daughter."

Several of the men grimaced.

The man laughed. "And you dumb fucks were gonna go hit on her? I almost would have paid money to see that shit. It would have been the show of the year once he found out."

Manuel scrubbed a hand down his face. "She looks older than she is. That's not fair."

Daryl snorted. "Don't fucking matter. You even think about sniffing her way, we all know what Brownstone would do. He'd pound your face into the cement like he did King Pyro or kick you through a window. And he'd be right to do it. I'd beat your asses if I had a daughter and you fuckers came around her."

Shorty gave a little salute. "Nothing but professionalism from me. I'm staying well away."

The men all laughed.

"No!" Alison shouted after James murmured something to her. She stamped her feet. "I shouldn't have to do this. It's not fair."

James snorted. "You're whining about a little exercise?" He waved a hand. "I've got to go talk to Charlyce about something. If you want to stay here and continue to have a tantrum, be my guest. If you want to go back home, start walking. It'll be good exercise." He spun and marched toward the door.

"You're such a jerk sometimes, Dad." Alison glared at the bounty hunter until he entered the building. "A real big jerk."

Shorty shrugged. "What should we do? Go ask Mr. Brownstone what to do?"

Daryl nodded toward the girl. "Nah. We know what he wants. We help her. It's obvious why he brought her here, you know what I'm saying? He said as much."

The men all nodded and marched as a group toward Alison. The girl stood there, arms crossed, still glaring at the door and muttering angry teenage barbs about her father.

Daryl approached Alison and gave her a polite nod. "Hey, Alison. I'm Daryl." He gestured to the gathered men. "We all work for your dad. This ain't all of us, but it's a good chunk of us. Welcome to the Brownstone Agency."

Alison sighed. "Sorry you all had to see that. Not my finest introduction."

"Hey, I didn't get along with my old man, either. But we're gonna help you out."

She blinked. "Help me out?"

"We're gonna help train the poor out of-shape-white girl." Daryl smirked. "That way your dad will get off your back."

Alison narrowed her eyes. "Just because I'm not some super-athlete doesn't mean I can't take care of myself. I'm tougher than I look." She lifted her chin and sniffed.

Daryl held up his hands. "Not saying you ain't, but we was all tough, too, real tough, but then your dad brought us in off the street, and with the help of the staff sergeant, he made us tougher. You can always get stronger, and getting stronger is all about being prepared. It's like the man said, 'To not prepare is the greatest of crimes; to be prepared beforehand for any contingency is the greatest of virtues.'"

Alison blinked. "My dad said that? It doesn't sound like him."

The bounty hunter laughed. "Nah. That sh…that stuff was from Sun Tzu, *The Art of War*. Our training's directed by Staff Sergeant Chris Royce, retired United States Marine Corps, but he ain't here today. He's big into stuff like Sun Tzu and Marcus Aurelius and all sorts of other old generals and warriors." He pounded his chest with a fist. "Strong heart, strong mind, strong body, you know what I'm saying? Physical training improves the others, and then at the end, you're a warrior."

The girl jerked her head from man to man, her eyes unfocused. The men didn't quite know what to make of it.

"I've got a strong heart, mind, and body already. I can take care of myself. I don't need your help."

Daryl shrugged. "Sure, sure, Alison. I bet you do a mean foot stomp. That'll scare people off."

Everyone laughed.

The girl smirked and lifted her hand. A purple flame winked into existence.

"Damn!" Manuel yelled. "She's a witch. We're gonna have fucking magical back-up now. Hell to the *yeah*."

Shorty smacked him on the back of the head. "Watch your mouth around Alison Brownstone, you fool."

More murmurs broke out, the men all staring at Alison's flame with interest.

Alison blinked and lowered her hand. "Um, I'm not technically a witch. I…" She waved a hand, and the flame disappeared. "Don't worry. It's complicated, but why aren't you scared? It's magic."

Daryl and Shorty exchanged a look, but it was Shorty who spoke. "Brownstone Agency is all about the reputation, you know what I'm saying? If we get scared and run from magic, it makes Mr. Brownstone look bad, and even though we handle the lower-level bounties, you never know what might pop up. We ran into a witch in Vegas not all that long ago. She beat our…" He coughed. "She had some good magic and we had some trouble with it, but we didn't run."

The rest all nodded their agreement.

Alison tilted her head and looked at Shorty, though her eyes still didn't seem to focus. Most of the men just thought it was some artifact of being magical.

Shorty slapped a hand on his chest. "Hey, in the end, we

are the Brownstone Agency. So that means we stand there and flip off wizards even if they're tossing lightning to kill us. We can't be running away like little punks just because someone's flashing magic. That's the world we live in now."

"Huh. Dad doesn't talk much about his work with me. He thinks I'll worry too much, but I like the concept. You guys are really brave."

The men all puffed out their chests. Every man liked a pretty girl telling them they were brave.

Daryl motioned toward the street. "We'll help you with a little run. It's gonna hurt, but getting stronger always hurts in the beginning."

Alison took a deep breath and nodded. "I can do this. I'll show my dad that I'm not some spoiled princess."

The bounty hunter jogged to the front, and the other men broke into two groups, one in front of Alison and the other behind her. She might not be a queen, but they were going to protect her like one.

***

Alison wasn't sure how much time had passed, only that her legs felt like rubber, her lungs burned, and her stomach was in open revolt against her brain. She collapsed to her knees as the group arrived back at the Brownstone Building and started puking.

"Get her some Gatorade, yo," Shorty shouted. "She looks dehydrated."

Manuel jogged off to get the drink.

The girl clutched her stomach and moaned. "I feel like I'm dying."

Daryl laughed. "At least you did better than Isaiah. Probably because you're skin and bones rather than having the spare tire around the middle like him."

"Hey!" Isaiah yelled from the back of the group. "I resemble that remark."

Alison took several deep breaths and sat up, again taking in the soul energy of the men. Beautiful souls. Yes, anger and other dark emotions lingered, but it was like their souls had begun to mirror her dad's. These were good men—hard men, but good men—being shaped into something even greater by James Brownstone.

The girl smiled, appreciating her soon-to-be adoptive father that much more.

Shay walked down the hallway toward the back of the Brownstone Building. James stood near a window, looking out with his arms crossed.

She moved closer to check outside. Alison was surrounded by James' men, her face and body covered in sweat as she struggled to finish another sit-up.

"This is your idea of a fun summer?" Shay asked.

James dropped his arms and shrugged. "Just being aware of threats and having magic isn't enough. She needs the fitness to win if someone does come after her."

The tomb raider chuckled. "While this looks fun and all, I think I'd rather work out in my own warehouse."

"Might do you some good to work in the heat."

Shay eyed him. "First of all, I've hit plenty of hot places on jobs. Besides, it's not even that hot yet."

James smirked. "Is that a no to sweating?"

The tomb raider shook her head. "I sweat in public when I'm getting paid. Otherwise, no reason, and I like my privacy." She nodded toward the window. "I'm still getting used to the idea of people knowing who I am." She stood on her tiptoes and kissed James. "Tell me how she does."

Shay turned and walked down the hallway.

"Before or after her bitching?" James called after her.

She looked over her shoulder. "Young girls don't bitch. They whine, complain, and try to get their way, but they don't get the Bitch Skill until they've been in a relationship long enough."

James stared as she walked away, trying to process what she'd just said.

Guess I'll have to ask the guys at the watering hole what the fuck that's supposed to mean.

The sweat dripping into Alison's eyes stung. She tried to blink it away as she climbed up the net, her legs and arms aching.

Stupid obstacle course. I can't believe he has me doing an obstacle course.

With a groan, the teen hit the top of the net and rolled onto her back on the raised wooden platform. She panted, trying to catch her breath and get her muscles working again. She still had several obstacles left.

From what her dad had told her, he'd gotten his hands on some lightly enchanted powder that he'd spread around the obstacle course, so at least it'd glow enough to her energy sight for her to have a chance of navigating it. She wasn't sure if his men knew she was blind or about her energy sight, but no one had commented on it, so she assumed they didn't.

Alison wasn't sure if she wanted to tell them. It was hard. People always reacted differently, and she didn't want them to pity her. She hated the exercise, but she liked that the men were being so nice and encouraging. She was so used to boys being afraid of the name Brownstone, but these men respected, rather than feared, her dad.

The guys had all zoomed through the obstacle course like it was nothing. Of course, they were trained bounty hunters and sighted.

"Come on, Alison," Shorty yelled from the other end. "You got this. Just dig deep, and keep pushing. Everyone hurts on the first try. Everyone wants to puke. You just got to tell the stomach to fu…uh, you got to tell it you're in charge, you know what I'm saying?"

Every part of her ached at this point, but she at least took some small comfort in knowing she had nothing left in her stomach to puke out. She had literally nothing left to lose.

Max clapped. "Yeah, do it, girl. You're still doing better than Isaiah did the first time."

Isaiah frowned at him. "Why do you got to do me like that?"

Several other cheers erupted from the gathered bounty hunters.

Alison pushed herself up and stood, taking several slow, deep breaths before jumping and grabbing the rope and flying over the mud below. She released on the other end, pride at her success adding energy to her step.

She hit a series of tires that forced her to adopt a wide stance, but the obstacle at least gave her upper body a rest. The girl concentrated on putting one leg in each tire and getting to the end of the obstacle. Only two more to go, and once she got over the final wall, the torture would be over, and she could rest.

I can do this. I've gone through scarier and harder things at school. I'll prove to Dad that I'm tougher than he thinks I am.

Alison gritted her teeth and dropped to her stomach, crawling under the barbed wire.

Seriously, Dad? Do you think the Drow are going to chase me under barbed wire?

She bit her lip as her face dragged along the sand. At least she hadn't been forced to do this in mud like she'd heard some of the men discussing.

The grueling moments passed, and Alison hopped to her feet, her heart pounding, her muscles twitching, and sweat practically gluing her clothes to her. She jogged toward the wall and rope that separated her from some well-earned rest.

The gathered bounty hunters clapped and cheered even louder.

"Come on, Alison. We see you. You've got this."

Almost there. So close. It's just so high.

The teen picked up her pace.

I'm not a normal person. I'm half-Drow, and I have magic. If someone were coming after me, I wouldn't not *use my magic. That would be dumb.*

Alison took several deep breaths and turned so the

crowd couldn't see her hands. She leapt toward the rope. A quick pulse of lavender erupted from her hands, and she shot up a few more feet.

She grabbed the rope, and with her aching and tired arms, crawled over the top and then slid down and released the rope. She sprawled on the ground on her back, her breathing hard.

James stood over her, his arms crossed, and shaking his head. "Now let's see you do it without the magic."

Alison groaned. "You saw that?"

He grunted. "I see everything."

"But why can't I use magic? It's part of what I am."

James shook his head. "It's useful, but you never know what might happen. At least if you can climb a wall without using magic, then, among other things, it means people looking for magic won't find you when you're scaling that wall. He nodded toward the course. "You're gonna do this again. We can talk about a magic-approved course once you've mastered this one."

Alison sighed and headed toward the first obstacle, her cheeks burning.

6

The next day, Alison was missing the obstacle course as she trudged toward the firing station at the indoor gun range in the Brownstone Building. Her heavy bulletproof vest made her movements awkward. It was obviously sized for one of her dad's grown bounty hunter men, so it was almost more a bulletproof dress than a bulletproof vest. It'd be funny in any other situation.

And he said this was one of the smaller ones.

She finished approaching the firing line and felt around until she found the pistol lying on the station. A target silhouette lay downrange. A light glow from sprinkled magic dust highlighted the target. This didn't feel like a cheat to her. At least in a normal situation, the energy of a person would be obvious, and she'd know exactly where to shoot.

Alison blew out a breath. Summer vacation had turned into boot camp.

Can't believe he's having me learn to shoot. I think I'd rather rely on my magic than guns, but it's not like he's going to let me skip shooting.

"Can you hear me?" James' voice came through a receiver in the bulky black electronic ear muffs protecting her hearing.

"Yes," Alison replied. She glanced at the bounty hunter, taking comfort in his beautiful soul. No matter how annoyed she might get with her dad, she knew that everything he was doing was only because he cared about her.

"The electronic ear muffs have active noise-canceling," James explained. "So you can take as many shots as you need without hurting your hearing. You'll still have the flash and recoil, but you're just training to shoot, not be a Marine, so I'm not all that worried about you running around hearing the shots go off or whatever. I've got something else planned to get you used to running and shooting, anyway."

The girl lifted up the gun, biting her lip. "I don't know about this, Dad."

James shook his head. "It's an equalizer."

"Huh? Is that what this type of gun is called?"

He chuckled. "No, it's a Glock, but my point is that in general, men are bigger than women. More upper-body strength too, which means if you get into a fistfight or something like that, you're gonna lose. And you're small, compared to most women. You need to work smarter, faster, and harder." He took a deep breath and slowly let it out. "Unlike a lot of people, you've seen the evil of our world. You know that it's not always some weird monster from Oriceran doing the worst stuff. So you understand that you need to be prepared."

Alison set the gun back down. "Not saying you're wrong, but what's that have to do with a gun being an equalizer?

"Don't you get it? Back in the day, even if a woman even *had* a knife or a sword, she was still at a disadvantage, because the men coming at her were bigger and stronger. A gun, especially a modern gun, doesn't care if you're bigger or stronger. That gun barely weighs anything, and it can take down a grown man with a single shot. They gave peasants guns, and they started killing knights. A leveler. An equalizer. A gun is a power you control through mental training as much as practice."

James whipped out his .45 and put three rounds downrange. Alison's electronic earmuffs killed almost all the sound. Though she could feel some of the vibration, her dad hadn't placed any magical powder on his target so she couldn't follow the attack, and she only knew he'd fired by following the glow of his energy in his arm. His weapon hadn't been coated with any magical powder either.

Wonder if he forgot? He's really getting into all this training stuff.

He grunted. "If you trained for years like Shay, then you could go one-on-one in hand-to-hand with a larger man, but you don't have to train for years with a gun for it to work."

Alison sighed. "I don't know if I could shoot someone, though."

"That's fine. It shouldn't be easy to kill someone, but at least you should practice. The more you practice, the less you have to think when the time comes."

The teen nodded and picked up the gun, holding it in

her hand for a moment to get a good sense for the heft and texture of the weapon. Could she kill someone? She'd said she couldn't, but at the same time, she couldn't deny the rage she'd felt when her mother was killed or when she'd thought her new dad might meet the same fate.

I should worry less about protecting myself and more about getting stronger so I can protect him. He didn't have to get involved. He could have let Walt drag me off to the Harriken. Then I'd be dead just like Mom. Or he could have turned me over to the Drow.

Alison took a shuddering breath.

He didn't have to take me in, and he doesn't have to adopt me. He's choosing to because he loves me.

She lifted the weapon and gripped it with both hands, staring downrange at the magical glow of the target.

Smarter, faster, harder. Her dad was right. She needed to improve every part of herself, from her body to her magic. It was the only way she'd never again lose someone she loved.

Alison pulled the trigger. The gun jerked in her hand, and she yelped.

James chuckled. "It's okay."

"Did...I hit?"

The bounty hunter pressed a button near Alison's station. The target buzzed as it moved toward her on an overhead track.

James inspected it for a few seconds. "Clipped him in the shoulder. Not bad for a blind girl."

Alison shrugged and set the gun down. "It'd be easier with an actual person. The soul would be brighter."

"Even if they were evil?"

The girl nodded. "It's the colors that are different, not the brightness. So, yeah, an evil guy would still be easy to spot."

She frowned. She'd run into more darkness than her dad needed to know.

"Good," James rumbled. "Go ahead and take off your ear protection. This was just about getting you used to handling the weapon."

Alison removed the ear muffs and hung them on a hook she'd felt earlier. James did the same.

The door to the range opened and Trey stepped into the room, a small bulletproof vest and tactical harness in hand. Alison only knew because they glowed under her energy sight.

"Enchanted armor?" she asked.

James shook his head. "Regular old vest and harness, but they are actually sized for you." He nodded to Trey. "Help her get them on."

Alison pulled off the heavy vest she had on and tossed it to the ground. She couldn't help but smile once the new vest and harness were on. Now that she didn't feel like a little girl wearing her daddy's clothing, she could appreciate what the armor and harness represented.

This training is tough, but he's helping me learn to take care of myself. I keep believing Dad thinks I'm just a little girl who always needs to be protected, but he wants me to be independent. He wants me to be strong.

She beamed a smile at Trey and James.

A few hours later, James stood outside, his arms crossed, watching as the entire bounty-hunting crew minus the Vegas team but including Trey, took on the obstacle course —this time in vests and tactical harnesses. Learning to move in a variety of situations with normal loadouts was vital. Royce had stressed it, as had James.

Maybe I should make them wear some of those gray coats that Shay hates so much.

Alison wasn't holding up the rear only because some of the men had purposely slowed to make sure they could help her if she needed it.

I'm spending a fortune on that magic dust so she can see, but I think it's worth it. She'll gain more confidence doing these obstacles than just normal exercise shit.

Royce walked over from the edge of the obstacle course to the bounty hunter. "Just to be clear, what do you want me to do with her?"

James arched an eyebrow. "I want you to train her like anyone else. Like any of the other men."

The drill instructor shook his head. "But she's not like the other men. She's got magic." He pointed to the girl as she jumped between logs. "Maybe all this physical training is a distraction."

"From what?" The bounty hunter grunted. "She goes to a magic school already. Nothing we're gonna be able to teach her there. Doesn't matter anyway. You know how this shit works. You can't assume you're always gonna have your best weapon working. She may have magic, but what if someone blocks it somehow?" He shook his head. "It's a dangerous world, and I want my daughter to not only be able to protect herself, but protect others."

Royce nodded slowly. "Makes sense. Hell, I'm interested to see what the Corps will do once magical people enlist in bigger numbers. All this shit is changing, and it's hard to know how it's gonna end up." He watched Alison move from a log obstacle to a net. "Protect others, huh? She going to follow you in the family business?"

"Don't know about that, but hell, she might have to protect *me* someday."

Royce laughed. "Seriously?"

"Yeah. You know my rep, and you've seen the kind of shit I have to deal with. She's like most kids. I love her, but she's also like a 401k plan. I invest in her, and I'll see benefits down the line." James shrugged at the other man. "If she's able to protect herself better, it'll lower my anxiety and help me focus. So, yeah, I want you to basically turn her into a little Marine with magic."

The other man grimaced. "Okay, you're the boss, but I'm going to throw you under the bus here."

"Huh?"

"I'm going to make it clear who's calling the shots about training. She won't hate me because I'm giving you all the glory."

James chuckled. "No problem. I've got broad enough shoulders to handle that shit."

Royce gave him a quick nod. "I've got to check something real quick before they finish the course. Be right back."

The bounty hunter waited until the man stepped inside to utter his final concern over the situation. "Shit, I *hope* I've got broad enough shoulders."

He looked up in time to see Alison reach the top of the net.

Tyler looked up from the bar as the front door opened. A teen girl with white-tipped black hair stepped through, and he frowned.

Come on. You think your weak-ass fake ID is going to fool me, kid?

He snorted. It'd been a while since he had a kid try and talk their way into booze at his place.

The Black Sun might be neutral ground, but he didn't want some annoyed soccer mom coming after him. They were scarier than the criminal scum he dealt with, and he doubted the cops would be all that happy with him serving minors.

A moment later, Brownstone stepped through the door and murmured something to the girl. She laughed and shook her head. They both walked toward the bar, navigating around tables and chatting Patrons. A few people glanced Brownstone's way but said nothing and didn't let their gazes linger too long, as if afraid they might earn his wrath just from looking at him.

Who the fuck is she? Oh, fuck, wait. I knew he had a kid he was looking after. That must be her. What was her name? Alison...yeah.

The bartender watched, eyes narrowed, as the bounty hunter and Alison approached the bar. He couldn't understand why he'd bring his underage soon-to-be adopted daughter to a bar filled with criminals and known for illegal gambling.

Tyler was proud of his place, but probably the only places less appropriate for minors in LA were brothels.

Alison reached out and ran her hand along the bar before dropping it to her side and finding a stool. She hopped on, and Tyler found himself staring. If he didn't know better, given what she'd just done and the distant look in her eyes, he might suspect she was blind, but the girl had managed to navigate through the room in front of Brownstone and to the bar without trouble.

Huh. Weird.

"You have Coke, right?" the girl asked. "Without the alcohol?"

Tyler nodded. "Yeah. We have Coke." He nodded to Brownstone as the man sat. "You think this is a good idea bringing her in here? There are a lot of bad people in here."

Alison nodded at her dad. "He's right, you know. I can see it. Pretty disgusting, a lot of them." She made a face.

The bartender laughed and set a glass filled with ice and a can of Coke in front of her. "Damn, girl. It's true, but maybe you shouldn't be saying it out loud."

Her cheeks reddened. "Sorry." She poured her soda into her glass and took a drink.

Brownstone grunted and shrugged. "If there's anyone stupid enough to try messing with her after seeing she's with me, it's gonna be a sad day for them. Plus, she can do stuff on her own. I'm not worried about her in here."

Tyler turned to grab a bottle of Irish Stout as he considered what that might even mean. Do stuff? Any daughter of Brownstone's probably was packing heat and ready to put bullets into people. The man just brought on too much trouble otherwise.

Or does he mean something else? She doesn't look that tough.

Brownstone's phone chimed, and he pulled it out of his pocket. His eyes narrowed as he read a text. "Call from the adoption lawyer." He looked up at Tyler. "I need to use your office so I can talk to him."

The bartender laughed. "What?"

"You heard me. I need to use your office. This shit is private."

"We have some sort of bromance now? You get to use my office…" Tyler's voice trailed off under the bounty hunter's heavy glare. "Man, too bad it's not Kathy's shift." He nodded toward the hallway leading to his office. "Fine. Just don't break anything."

Brownstone hopped off his stool. "I'll try not to, but no promises." He turned to Alison. "Stay here. I'll be right back."

The girl smiled as the bounty hunter wandered into the back.

She turned her attention toward Tyler, her slightly unfocused gaze unnerving him.

Is she playing mind games on me? Is this some sort of Brownstone family double-team?

"This is the famous Black Sun, huh?" the girl commented.

"Famous?"

Alison nodded. "My dad's told me a little about it." She smirked. "He's also told me you've made a lot of money off him."

Tyler shrugged. "I'm a businessman, first and foremost,

and your father is a good investment. Nothing more, nothing less."

Her smile disappeared. "Yeah, like when he and you came up with that stupid plan to have him fight a scheduled bounty?"

The bartender took a deep breath and slowly let it out. The last thing he wanted to do was go over the damned fight promotion plan again. Maria wouldn't ever let him begin to forget about it. He only shrugged.

A loud thump caught his attention as a small crew of four twenty-something guys in too-slick shirts and pants strolled into the Black Sun. Their smirking expressions adorned punchable faces as they strolled up to the bar.

The first man grinned and looked around. "You see this? We're in *the* Black Sun. I'm amazed we haven't been knifed already."

The night is young, asshole.

One of his friends laughed. "You're so right, Brock."

Tyler sighed and shook his head. Nothing worse than slumming out-of-neighborhood tourists. "What can I get for you gentlemen?"

Brock licked his lips and looked Alison up and down. "Look at you, hot thing."

Oh, fuck. Don't, asshole. Just don't. Even if you're not a criminal, Brownstone is gonna punt you into fucking orbit.

Alison rolled her eyes. "Please. If you could see what I can see, you'd know why I'd never give you the time of day."

One of the friends laughed. "Ouch. Talk about getting shot down."

Brock snorted. "You think you're something? Because

you hang out at this place?" He sneered. "Oh, I get it. You're the kind of chick who gets off on being around criminals and scumbags. I can show you what a real man with a real job is like."

Tyler searched the bar for any cops, but his typical luck prevailed. Nothing but criminals in the crowd. He'd need to intervene for the girl's safety and the continuing existence of his bar.

"Now wait one—" Tyler began before stopping at Alison's raised hand.

The girl hopped off the stool and smiled. "A real man, huh?"

A huge grin split Brock's face. "That's right, baby. I'll show you something you will never forget."

Alison leaned forward and reached toward his crotch. "Like this?"

"Damn. Yeah, that's right. Slow it down."

The girl reached forward and stopped a few inches in front of Brock's pants. She smiled. "Or how about this?"

A purple flash erupted from her hand. Brock yowled and stumbled backward, the crotch of his pants blackened and smoking.

Tyler stared at him, his brain taking a while to understand what was going on before he winced.

Brock danced around, holding himself. "Son of a fucking bitch. Oh, fuck. You stupid bitch."

Tyler glared at the man. "Get out now."

"That bitch just burned my dick, man!"

"Don't make me ask again." Tyler frowned and wondered if he'd need to go for his gun to make his point. He prided himself on not having to rely on petty threats of violence, but these assholes weren't from the local scene. They didn't understand the subtle rules that defined a place like the Black Sun.

Fucking civilians.

Brock's friends squared their shoulders and stepped in front of their wounded friend.

Several large men on either side of them stood, including Ralph.

"Black Sun is neutral ground, boy," the thug growled. He loomed over the men. "And you don't go attacking the bartender. Who the fuck is supposed to give us our drinks?"

Alison rolled her eyes and crossed her arms.

Brock panted in his pain, and his friends looked around at the angry men surrounding them.

Ralph smirked. "That's Alison Brownstone. Even if you managed to beat her, you think you can beat her dad?"

"Let's get the fuck out of here," Brock shouted. "This place is full of cunts anyway." He hurried toward the door, wincing with each step.

His friends followed him out, with one holding up his middle finger.

Ralph and the other patrons sat down once the assholes had exited the building.

Alison sat back down on a stool. "What a jerk."

Tyler stared at the door for a moment before nodding. "That was an interesting trick. That something Brownstone taught you?"

She shook her head and took another sip of Coke before replying. "That wasn't from Dad. It's from my mom."

"Well, in any event. Thanks."

"Thanks?"

Tyler nodded. "Yeah. If you hadn't taken care of them so quickly, your dad might have come out and seen what was up. I don't know what kind of father Brownstone is, but I know the kind of bounty hunter he is, and I figure this would have ended with my front door being broken from Brownstone throwing them through it."

Alison blinked. "Seriously?"

"Yeah, seriously." He pointed toward the door. "Yeah, your dad came in here after a bounty once. The guy was a pretty serious thug. He wasn't about to give up just because James Brownstone told him to. The fight pretty much started with your dad throwing him through my door."

"He really did that?" The teen laughed.

"Yeah."

Alison smiled. "It does kind of sound like him. Sorry about that."

Tyler shrugged. "At least he paid for the door."

James emerged from the hallway, a deep scowl on his face.

The bartender's stomach tightened. Maybe Brownstone knew what had happened and was about to go run the men down.

I hope the fuckers are already out of my parking lot. Don't need bodies there.

The bounty hunter walked over toward Alison. He scrubbed a hand over his face and sighed. "I thought that was the lawyer calling to say everything was finalized, but it turns out there's a small issue."

Alison frowned. "Issue?"

"Yeah, the State of California is fighting the adoption. We've got to go to court. Something about your Oriceran heritage making things different, but mainly because I'm a bounty hunter, they say that I can't provide a good home environment for someone with your unique background." He snorted. "It's like they think I'm prejudiced against Oricerans or some killer thug."

Oriceran heritage? That explains the trick and the weird hair. So the girl's magical. Huh.

The teen swallowed. "What's that mean? Are they going to take me?"

James shook his head and gritted his teeth. "No one's gonna take you. I won't let them. I don't give a shit if they are the government."

Tyler frowned but remained silent. He didn't always care for Brownstone, but he didn't like the idea of the government coming in and screwing with a man trying to adopt a kid. Oriceran shouldn't make a difference.

"Come on, Alison," the bounty hunter rumbled. He stomped toward the door, and the teen followed him, a defeated look on her face.

Tyler could only watch.

A few minutes later, Maria stepped into the building and made her way to the bar. For once, she didn't look like she wanted to stab Tyler when she sat on a stool.

"Hey," Tyler offered. He poured her a drink and set it in front of her. The cop was out of uniform, so he figured it was time for some hard liquor.

Maria gulped down half the glass. "Hey."

"I didn't hear anything about any AET showdowns today."

She shrugged. "Things have been slow. That's a good thing." She blew out a breath. "Look, I'm still miffed, but I can't stay mad at idiocy forever or I'll never be happy, especially considering all the idiots I have to deal with at work."

Tyler shrugged. "Glad to hear that." He glanced back up at the door. "Hey, maybe this isn't something you'd know about, but you've got connections. You know anything about the government trying to block Brownstone's adoption because the girl's part-Oriceran and because he's a bounty hunter?"

Maria furrowed her brow and shook her head. "I knew he had a girl he was trying to adopt, and that her dad was a piece of shit Brownstone took down, but I didn't know she was part-Oriceran. I'll ask around, though. That sounds like some bullshit. Like saying an American can't adopt a kid just because he's from another country." She snorted. "That's the government for you."

"Says the cop." Tyler smirked.

She narrowed her eyes. "Yeah, *now* I remember why I was mad at you."

7

James paced his living room floor, his fists clenched and his pulse pounding in his ears. Alison was in her room. She claimed she was tired from the long day of training, but the look of pain on her face haunted the bounty hunter.

I was supposed to protect her, and the fucking government is coming at me? This is complete bullshit.

"Those fuckers," he growled. "How fucking dare they. Hasn't she been through enough pain? Don't they give a shit about her suffering?"

The bounty hunter took several deep breaths. The complexity of the situation was helpful in that it'd kept him from marching somewhere to kick down doors. He didn't know who to beat up or threaten to solve the problem, which meant he had to rely on his lawyer.

He pulled out his phone and dialed Shay.

"What's up?" she answered.

"I have to go to court," James rumbled. "Those fuckers are making me go to court. Can you believe this shit?"

Shay laughed. "After all these years of doing your thing, someone finally has the balls to sue you? I'm only surprised it took this long. It's not a big deal. The way the laws are written, as long as they were a legal bounty, it's hard to win in court."

"Not that." He growled. "The state is trying to block my adoption of Alison."

Shay's tone turned serious. "What the fuck? Are you kidding me?"

"They say because she's half-Oriceran and because I'm a bounty hunter with a history of 'extreme violence and an unstable home environment' that I'm not a good fit. That I can't provide for a child of her unique familial needs." James sucked in a breath. "Fuck them with a rusty nail, every last one of them."

"Yeah, fuck those assholes. You're gonna fight them, aren't you?"

"Hell, yes, I'm gonna fight them. There's no way I'm letting them take Alison from me." James glared at the wall, wishing he had a punching bag to demolish. "I'll do whatever I need to. I don't give a shit if it's the government I'm against. I'm gonna protect Alison."

Shay sighed. "Okay, I get that you're pissed, and I'm pissed too, but you still have to keep a clear head about this. Promise me you won't do anything stupid, okay?"

"Like what?"

"Meaning, you can't throw the first punch. They already have this idea that you're some dangerous out-of-control bounty hunter, and it sounds like that's what's mainly fueling this. If you give them any reason to believe that, you'll lose this." Shay inhaled sharply. "I wouldn't even be surprised if they eventually start *trying* to get you to blow up. This might be some petty asshole mad at you because you're famous."

James stopped pacing and dropped to his couch. "I understand when not to fight, and it's not time—*yet.* I'll let the lawyer do his thing before I start thinking about kicking down doors."

Shay let out a sigh of relief. "Good. Now go talk to her about it. She needs to know you've got her back."

"Huh? She knows about it." James glanced toward the stairs. "I told her right away."

"But have you really talked about it?" Shay sighed. "Told her not just that you're gonna fight it, but everything about how you feel about this and her."

"No, I haven't." The bounty hunter grunted.

"Go do that now. She's a scared teen who is probably thinking she's gonna lose her new dad just when she thought everything was finally gonna be over."

James rubbed the back of his neck. "Can I call you if I need help? I'm not good at a lot of this emotional shit."

Shay let out a pained chuckle. "Sure, but you need to start understanding how to deal with your teen daughter without me around as a translator. Okay? Even after you handle this situation, this won't be the last crisis."

"Fine. Talk to you later, then."

James ended the call and slipped the phone back into his pocket. After a deep breath, he headed up the stairs toward Alison's room and knocked on the door.

Fuck. I wish I could just go find someone to punch in the damned face and end this.

"Come in," she called from inside.

James opened the door and stepped inside. The girl lay on her back on her bed with a pained look on her face. Her eyes were puffy from tears.

He sighed. "You doing okay, kid?"

Alison rolled to face him. "They're going to take me, aren't they? They aren't like the Harriken. They're the government."

"Hell no, they aren't gonna take you. We're gonna to fight this, and we're gonna win." James grunted. "I've faced down necromancers, the Drow, Harriken, and weird-ass despair monsters. I'm not afraid of a few lawyers and judges. Screw them if they think they can take my daughter from me."

"But what if we *can't* win? What if they say you can't be my dad?"

James marched over to the bed and sat beside her. "They don't get to make that decision."

"But don't they? I mean, that's the whole point of this."

He shook his head. "It doesn't matter who says what. Unless *you* say otherwise, I'm going to be your dad, and if they try to fight that, I'll fight harder until they give up. You know me. I'm straightforward, and I like to keep things simple. And occasionally I like to blow things up to make my point."

Alison managed a light chuckle, but her smile disappeared, and she swallowed. "I was thinking earlier that we do have a back-up plan if we lose in court. Something to keep in mind."

James frowned. He didn't want her scheming about fleeing to Mexico. "We don't need a backup plan. We're gonna win in court and make them sorry they ever tried to challenge this adoption."

"But if we don't, then we need a plan, and I have a plan. That's all I'm saying." Alison shrugged.

"Okay, Alison, what's your plan?"

The girl took a deep breath. "The wish. Maybe if we used it, it'd make the whole problem go away without you beating anyone up or destroying buildings."

James shrugged. "Maybe, but it could have effects we don't even know about. We need to be careful about how and when we use it. And are you sure you want to use it for something like this?"

"Yes. I'd rather lose the wish than lose you." Alison sniffled and wiped away a fresh tear.

James pulled her into a hug. "And that's why I still have it. It's a decent plan, but the situation isn't bad enough yet. We can do this. We can fight and win, and your mother will know that we didn't just cheap out against someone coming at us."

He nodded. They would fight, and they would fucking win.

***

James sat on his couch reading through the latest barbeque news, desperate for a distraction. He wanted to get ready to fight the adoption case, but this was one time where being a bounty hunter with an alien amulet wouldn't help him. He'd have to rely on the adoption lawyer's advice. He didn't like feeling helpless. Not one damned bit.

There was a light knock on the door. James stood and

marched over there, slipping his phone into the pocket. He wasn't surprised. He'd already scheduled a meeting before he'd been hit with the news about the adoption. Canceling the meeting was a possibility, but sitting around brooding wouldn't do him any good. Shay was also supposed to come by soon to take Alison out to get her mind off things with some girl time, but for now, the teen remained in her room skimming the web with the help of her haptic reader.

James didn't expect Shay, though. Not yet.

The bounty hunter opened the door. Mack stood on the other side.

"Hey, Mack," James rumbled. He gestured inside.

The police sergeant headed to the couch and took a seat. "You sure you want to do this right now?"

The bounty hunter turned and frowned. "What are you talking about?"

"There's been talk about your situation at the station. I heard that the state's trying to screw with your adoption."

James shrugged and sat in a recliner. "Yeah. They are. They say I'm not a good fit for a girl like Alison."

"You need anything, you let me know. I'll write you a whole novel full of recommendations if you need it. More than a few cops at the station will. You should talk to your priest and anyone who works at the orphanage, too. That's got to count for something."

"I'll let you know, but I don't want to talk about that shit now." James grunted.

"Yeah, I feel you. We can talk about the pit if you want." Mack grinned. "Nothing makes a man feel better than discussing the preparation of a little mouth-watering barbeque."

"We settled on something that we can carry using my truck, right?"

The cop nodded. "Yeah, a super-huge pit would be too much to manage, and we're going more with wood? I think that's a good, strong idea, but I can be persuaded otherwise."

"That was the plan." James furrowed his brow. "So I'm thinking at least partial vent-based temperature control. That's something we can get across to the guys without too much trouble, and they can learn to do it well."

"Yeah, sounds easy enough. Maybe we should have different specialists for low and slow vs. hot and fast. That kind of thing."

James shook his head. "I don't know. I'm more of a low and slow guy in general, but you're right. It might not hurt. Maybe we get two or three pits. Hell, I can get more than one truck." He furrowed his brow. "Or is this making shit too complicated already?"

Mack shrugged. "Your call in the end, since it's your men and you're paying the bills, but I think we can do a lot with one pit. It's not like every guy will be at every competition, you know?"

"True enough." James nodded slowly, the desire to maximize barbeque possibilities losing against his natural inclination toward simplicity. "One large-but-not-giant pit, then. That's a good start."

"Agreed." Mack looked over to the stairs where Alison was making her way down. "Hey, Alison."

"Hey, Sergeant Mack," she called back. She smiled at James. "Aunt Shay sent me a text to say she was on her way, and she'd be out front in a few minutes. I was going to go wait out there if it's okay."

James shrugged. "Fine by me. Not like my front porch is dangerous."

At least not these days.

Mack grinned. "You don't want to talk about making barbeque?"

Alison shrugged. "I think I'll just get it from a local BBQ place or have my Dad make it."

He winced and looked at James. "Guess you're going to need a son to carry on your legacy."

"It's not about that." Alison pointed to her eyes. "I can't see too well, so I'd be mostly guessing on the meat. Besides, who wants to smell like smoke?"

After a light knock on the door, the girl headed over and opened it.

Shay nodded to her Fiat, which was still running. "Ready to go?"

"Yeah, I'm ready." Alison smiled. "Thanks for this."

"No problem." Shay turned and walked toward her car.

James watched the women depart and shook his head. "Just can't get either of them interested in barbeque. It's not like they hate it, but they don't appreciate the subtlety and possibilities."

Mack clapped him on the shoulder. "It's all right, Brownstone. You've got a whole team of guys to share your passion now. Not like my wife loves all my hobbies."

Shay licked her chocolate ice cream cone. Alison sat across from her working on her mint chocolate chip. She was almost finished.

It's like she's starved for ice cream, the way she's going at that cone.

"How is your cone?" the tomb raider asked. "Do they even have ice cream at that school of yours?"

Alison laughed. "Yes, they have ice cream. It's a magic school, not a jail. I just really like this ice cream, is all."

"Jail, huh? You can learn valuable skills in jail." Shay licked her cone again. "But some skills we can learn without having to go that far."

"What do you mean?"

"If James gets to do all this training nonsense, then I want to have a little fun, too." Shay shrugged.

Alison blinked. "Meaning what, exactly? Am I going to regret coming out with you?"

Shay waved a hand. "Don't worry, I know how to make this all fun. We're gonna play a little game at the mall here after we're done with our ice cream. A situational awareness game."

"A situational awareness game?"

"Yep." Shay set her cone on her napkin on the table. "You failed my little test with the bug, but I have a few other little tags I want to play around with. Not true tracking devices, just a training thing. This time they won't be magical, so it's not just a matter of you using your sight to find their auras." She smirked. "Not that it helped last time."

Alison frowned. "That doesn't seem very fair."

"Good. Assholes are rarely fair, and I'm training you to deal with assholes."

An old woman wandering by shot a glare at the table but hurried away when Shay offered her a cold stare.

Once their audience was gone, Shay returned her attention to Alison. "I went out and grabbed a prepaid credit card loaded up with a nice amount of money. You can use it to buy ten things at the mall. I'm going to watch you, and if I can tag you, you have to return the item. I'll only try to tag once per item."

"You'll tag the thing I bought, then?"

Shay shrugged. "Maybe. The only real hint I'm gonna give you is that I'm gonna tag the stuff in order. You have until you enter the next store to find it, but that's all you get out of me. In a real-world situation, you don't always know how your enemy is going to try and bug you."

"This doesn't seem so hard after all." Alison nodded, a confident smile spreading over her face. "Wait, it's easier than I thought. All I have to do is just go immediately to the next store."

"Sure." Shay snickered. "That also means you have less time to find it if I've already planted the tag."

"Oh." Alison frowned. "I can do this. You only got me when I came in because I wasn't expecting anything. What about the final tag? What's the time limit?"

"No time limit," Shay replied. "The final tag will be the ultimate test. You'll need to make it all the way back to the mall entrance."

Alison clapped once. "This will be the easiest training of the last few days."

"Find my tags first, and then you can say that."

8

Alison smiled and handed the card to the cashier. The woman ran it and handed it back, the girl aware only because she could follow the movements of the woman's energy. The teen moved her hand to the location of the card and slipped it back into her pocket.

Her dad had been right. Sometimes it was easier if she admitted she was blind, and even with her energy sight strengthening with the increase in her magic, she was still at a major disadvantage. She hadn't even told most of her friends at school.

But telling people didn't appeal to her. She'd been independent for a long time, and the last thing she needed was anyone feeling sorry for her.

It was one of the reasons she'd stopped being angry at her dad for his harsh training regimen. If she were more fit, she could be more independent.

Alison picked up the bag containing the sweater she'd purchased more for texture than appearance. She could only wonder what it actually looked like, but the cashier hadn't made any comments to suggest it was ugly.

You're not going to win, Aunt Shay. I've got this. I know exactly what your soul looks like, and I'll spot you if you get close.

The teen laughed as she carried the bag out of the store and took a deep breath. She pulled out her modified phone and brought up the assistive voice map app. Fortunately, the mall had an up-to-date map database to interface with the program. Things would be even easier than she thought.

"You are currently outside of Lana's Dresses," a soft female voice reported. "You are across from Outrageous Shoes and More. Please say a command for more information or additional options."

"End readout," Alison announced. She slipped the phone back into her pocket. If she hurried over to the shoe store, that wouldn't give Shay a lot of time to slip one of her tags into the girl's things.

You're here right now watching me, aren't you?

Alison scanned the crowd, the mix of the crowd's energies not as confusing as they would have been before she started going to the School of Necessary Magic. She dealt with a lot of people at school, and she'd gotten far more used to picking out unique energy patterns. Her increased magic also seemed to make it easier.

Unfortunately, a careful check didn't locate Shay or anyone else who appeared to be waiting and hanging around the area near her.

You've got a plan. I just have to figure it out.

Alison turned, and a large man bumped into her.

"Oof."

She almost fell, but quickly regained her footing.

"Sorry about that," the man offered.

She shrugged. "No problem. I didn't even drop anything."

"Okay. Again, really sorry about that." He continued on his way.

I can't just keep standing around here. Shay's probably already closing on me to drop the tag.

Alison walked toward the shoe store. There was no magical energy for her to perceive to mark the entrance to the store, but it was easy to establish the entrance by paying attention to the energy of the people inside and outside the store and their relative positions.

She stepped into the shoe store, the warmth of triumph spreading through her.

Too easy. You didn't even get close, Aunt Shay.

Her phone rang. She ran her finger across the dynamic Braille display. Shay was calling.

"Yes?" Alison answered. "Impressed yet?"

Shay snorted. "Check the sweater."

The girl reached inside the bag and ran her hand over the sweater. A hard, thin bar was clipped to it. She sighed.

"You're kidding me."

Shay chuckled. "Here's how we'll do this, I'll return everything for you after we're done with the little game, so you're not wasting too much time in between. Plus, I like the idea of you being forced to carry bags you'll have to get rid of as a sort of penalty."

"How did you even get that in there? I know what your soul energy looks like. There's no way you snuck up on me.

Was it the guy? Did you hire him, and he did some pick-pocket stuff?"

Shay laughed. "A magician never reveals her secrets. You're zero for one, kid. Not a good start, but you've got nine more chances to prove yourself."

Alison shook her head. "Don't worry. This battle has just begun."

The teen crept along slowly, taking deep breaths as she surveyed the thick crowd. She was on item five, a new haptic Braille reader. Her old one worked well enough, but the new item would be easier to interface with her existing phone.

Her heart pounded in her chest as the energy of the people nearby blurred together. She was zero for four, and she'd yet to even get a glimpse of Shay.

How is she doing this? She said they wouldn't be magic, so she's not teleporting them. Plus, if she were using a spell like that, I'd see the energy.

Alison took a few deep breaths to try to calm her heart rate. She couldn't believe she was being beaten so badly. Sure, Shay had way more life experience at this sort of thing, but Alison thought her soul and energy sight would be more than enough to make up for the difference.

Guess this was what Dad was getting at when he was talking about not always being able to rely on magic.

She shook her head.

I've been rushing things. That's my problem. I should take my time and look for the tag. I have until the next store.

Alison moved to the side of the flow of foot traffic and started rooting around her latest bag for any sign of the tag. The last four had all been on the item directly, and easy to find once Shay called her.

Nothing. Shay hadn't made her move yet.

I can still win this round.

The teen stood and continued toward the next store with the help of the assistive map. She arrived at the store but didn't step inside. Instead, she again checked the bag and the box for the reader.

Nothing.

Alison quickly looked all around her. There was no sign of Shay.

I win this one. Ha!

With a grin, the girl stepped into the store. She almost cackled when her phone rang.

"Hello, Aunt Shay, guess you fo—"

"There's a little something on your shoe."

Alison blinked and knelt to feel along her shoe. A now-familiar hard thin bar lay atop it.

"That's impossible," she grumbled. "There's no way. You said these weren't magic. Is that true?"

"Yep. Not magic. Now, there's a bit of tech involved, won't deny that, but no magic." Shay chuckled. "Zero for five. We're heading into the back half, Alison. Better up your game. I'd hate to have a shut-out, especially when you told me how easy you thought this was gonna be."

The setting sun forced James to turn on the living room lights, but the last few hours had been well-spent, in his opinion.

Mack yawned and stretched. "So we're agreed, then. We've got those different recipes and ideas you wanted to try, but we're sure about the pit."

James grunted. They'd gone back and forth a few times, and he was reminded why he'd tried to live his life using KISS. The minute he'd started thinking about complicated variations for his beloved barbeque, everything had fallen apart, and he'd started second-guessing himself.

"Yeah," the bounty hunter finally managed. "We're good."

Mack grinned. "It's going to be damn sweet. Pull-behind, eight wheels on the back with two by two on each side. A hitch for hauling, built-in adjustment for leveling. This thing's going to be the nicest damned pit you can have without actually needing a big rig."

"Still tempted by that, to be honest."

"Nah, we're right to keep it this way. Otherwise, there might be competitions we can't enter." Mack shrugged. "You read the whole email I sent you when you were in the bathroom, right? I mean, based on what I found on the website earlier, this thing's not going to be cheap."

James nodded. "Yeah, I know. It's not like I have better shit to spend my money on than a barbeque pit. I'll put in the order once I've talked to the accountant. This is for the Brownstone Agency, not a personal thing."

Mack laughed. "Yeah, I love how you're about to drop so much money on barbeque equipment, yet still going to figure out a way to pay fewer taxes."

"I don't give that much of a shit, but my accountant keeps telling me to pay more attention to when I can write shit off."

Mack stood and stretched. "I better get going pretty soon, or my wife might be chopping *me* up to make into barbeque."

James chuckled. "It's been nice talking to you, Mack. I needed the distraction."

"I meant what I said earlier, Brownstone. A lot of us at the station have your back, and that shit includes AET now, even if Hall still is sore about your little streaming stunt."

"Thanks, Mack. I appreciate it. I'll let you know, depending on what the lawyer says."

The cop gave him a final nod and headed for the door. He frowned, stopped, and turned around. "Oh, I almost forgot to ask you. A woman named Heather contacted me about my rental unit. Claims you as a reference. I'm thinking that's a gutsy move if she's lying."

James shook his head. "She's not lying. She does some contract work for me at times. She's got a young kid, and she's looking to relocate to Los Angeles, and live somewhere she feels safe."

"Feels safe?"

The bounty hunter nodded. "She's had bad experiences in San Francisco. I figure living in a cop's place will make her feel a little more relaxed. She's in a wheelchair, too."

Mack grinned. "Luckily I got that ramp installed back when I thought my mother-in-law was going to be stuck in a wheelchair and wanted to live with us. At least now it doesn't feel like such a waste of money."

James chuckled. "Sounds like it'd be perfect for Heather and her son, then."

Yeah." Mack opened the front door. "If she's good enough for James Brownstone, she's good enough to rent from me."

"Thanks," James replied. "She might not be able to move in for a month. She has a few things to take care of first."

"Fine by me. I'm in no hurry." The cop waved, stepped outside, and closed the door behind him.

James looked around the empty house, frowning. With his friend gone, the looming threat of the court hearing returned. There was only one thing left for a man who'd spent hours discussing barbeque to do.

Fuck it, I'm gonna go get some ribs.

***

Okay, calm down, Alison. It doesn't matter that you're zero for eight. You've got this. Shay's not gonna get your new memory foam pillow.

The girl looked back and forth, her back against a wall as she looked for Shay's familiar soul. She hadn't caught sight of the woman directly the entire time in the mall, but there were so many people it was hard to be sure. She'd been too confident.

She probably is getting close, though. If she was launching the tags from two hundred feet away it'd defeat the purpose of what she's trying to teach me. It's supposed to be about immediate situational awareness that doesn't rely on any magic other than my energy sight.

Alison tried to consider possible clues. She'd been

bumped into four times. One or two times was one thing, but not four, especially when she was going out of her way to avoid people. After the first two times, she'd checked the latest bag and her clothes for a tag and found nothing, so it wasn't like the people themselves were planting the tags. If they weren't accidents, then the question remained of why they were bumping into her.

Distraction seemed the obvious explanation.

The teen nodded and tried to channel her inner Shay. Alison couldn't see the tags, but she could see people. It apparently wasn't important to take her attention away from the item, but rather the person planting the tags, and somehow Shay was accomplishing that a different way the four bump-free times.

Shay's distracting me from her. She must be watching me, then gets close when she has the person bump into me so I don't notice her. If she's going that far, she must be darn close when it happens.

Alison nibbled on her lip as she made her way toward the final store, staying close to the wall so she had less area to examine. She slowed her pace and took a moment to check her pillow, and then the rest of her body. Still no tags.

It was just a few more yards to the store. A man bumped into her, but Alison ignored him, instead looking the opposite way. Familiar soul colors emerged from the crowd, and the teen offered Shay a wave.

Got you.

Shay turned and walked the opposite way. Alison took the chance to head into the candle shop to buy the aromatherapy candle set she wanted.

Alison had caught a glimpse of Shay's energy a few times, but the woman kept disappearing back into the crowd. Nobody else had bumped into her during the minutes it'd taken her to walk from the candle shop toward the front of the mall, which meant Shay was going to use her other strategy.

I'm onto you now. I'm going to win this last round.

Following the flow of people to the entrance was easy, but unlike with many of the shops, a faint residue of magic was embedded in the front doors of the mall. Whether it was something the owners of the building had done or the result of something unrelated Alison didn't know, but that still made it far easier to judge the exact distance to the exit.

The teen slowed her pace and moved against a wall to do a tag check on her body and candles. Nothing.

Alison swallowed, set her bags down, and wiped her sweaty palms. She did another quick inspection of the candle bag and her clothes for a tag.

Given her position along the wall with only a few yards to the exit and Shay nowhere in sight, she was home free. She couldn't imagine a way the woman could plant the tag. Sure, the tomb raider had been watching Alison, but now she couldn't get close enough to plant a tag, and another distraction stunt with someone bumping into her was bound to fail. Shay would just have to watch Alison stroll out of the building.

The girl frowned. No, that'd be too easy. If Shay had

been watching her the entire time, then that meant she also could easily figure out what direction she was going.

She gasped. That was the key.

She said they weren't magical, but she didn't say they weren't gadgets. Maybe they bounce onto me when I get close. If they're already on the ground, no one might notice them.

Alison took a deep breath and slowly let it out. No wonder Shay had been getting her. The teen had been too predictable in her walking paths.

She looked to her side, watching the flow of energy and people and waiting for her chance. A few seconds ticked by, and Alison sprinted for the exit on the opposite side, darting between a few people while she headed for the doors.

A few people yelled at her, but the girl reached the door without a collision. She threw it open and stepped outside.

Her heart pounding, Alison waited for Shay to call.

Instead, the woman stepped out of the door across the way and headed toward the teen. Alison tilted her head, not sure for once if the soul she was seeing was Shay's, but when the woman drew closer, she no longer had any doubts.

"Two for ten," Shay commented. "Not great, but it wasn't zero, so it's a good start."

Alison smiled. "Thanks, Aunt Shay."

"Let's do a little debrief before we head to the car. First of all, did you have some sort of strategy? It seems like you figured out things toward the end."

"Not really a strategy." Alison shrugged. "The only thing is that I grabbed stuff in the order I wanted it, so I figured I'd get the things I wanted most toward the end."

"Wait, so what you wanted most were a new pillow and some candles?"

The girl nodded.

Shay sighed. "I don't know if that's great or sad. Okay, just to make sure you weren't lucking out, tell me a little about your mindset on the last couple of items."

Alison nodded. "Okay, well, I realized you were sending distractions at times, so I wanted to reduce the amount of area I had to search. That's why I kept sticking to the wall."

"Good thinking, though can you think of a tradeoff?"

Alison furrowed her brow. "Even though there were fewer places to watch me from, there were fewer places I could run."

"Exactly. No perfect strategies. And the last bit?"

The teen glanced back at the light magical glow of the doors. "I kept assuming before that you were sneaking up on me, but at the last minute I realized you were setting traps."

Shay nodded. "Good thinking, Alison. Yeah, people after you won't always use the same strategy. From what we can figure out, the Drow first tried deception on James, and then they used brute force. Adapt and overcome." She walked over to pull Alison into a tight hug. "There just might be some hope for you yet."

9

———————

Several days later, Alison stood outside the tactical room as James helped zip her jumpsuit.

"You sure about this, Dad?"

"Yeah. You've been doing really well lately," James offered. "And the guys all like you and respect that you're trying hard. This is just a continuation of your training. Remember, they aren't real guns."

Alison smiled and stepped back. "I can't say I'm crazy about doing all that exercise, but at least I'm not puking at the end anymore." She frowned. "I feel like I'm lying to everybody, though. They don't know that I can't see. It feels kind of rude given, how nice they're treating me."

James shrugged. "It's a lesson for them as well. They need to learn to pick up on hidden body language. If they ask, you can tell them the truth. Until then, it's on them to figure it out." He handed her a rifle simulator. "A bounty hunter should never ignore obvious clues."

Alison could see the slight outline of the weapon, and since she doubted her dad was using fake magic rifles, she could only assume he'd been messing around with the magical powder again.

"Remember, it's not real, but it's gonna hurt. That pain is real enough," James explained. "But it'll hurt less if you go down. Also, remember you're on the blue team."

She shrugged. "I know, but Dad, that's pretty useless for me. Not like I can see the color of their uniforms."

The bounty hunter leaned in and handed her a small earbud. "Yeah, I know, need to make it fair. If you aim at someone and press the auxiliary button on the simulator, it'll beep if they are on the enemy team. It's not automatic, though, so you can't use it like some sort of general enemy team sensor. Or you can always just fire. There's no friendly fire setting for this set of training matches. That'll make it easier for all of you."

The teen nodded. "If I'm close enough I can recognize their energy, and I know who is on the other team. Won't they figure out I'm blind pretty quickly with me having to stumble through all the ramps and obstacles and blocks?"

James shook his head. "Shay and I coated the entire place with more of the magical powder I bought from Zoe. It doesn't do anything, but it *is* magical, so you'll be able to make out the entire place, just like with the obstacle course."

"How much did that cost, Dad? It seems like half this place is coated in that powder. Even if it's useless, it's still magic."

"Don't worry about it. It's not like I have anything better to do with my money." James shrugged. "Look, I get that in the real world you won't necessarily have that advantage, but you need to learn weapons handling in movement and cover situations to even have a chance." He frowned. "Maybe I could buy a ton of this powder, and you could carry some around and coat places if you get in trouble."

Alison laughed. "I'm not carrying around a bunch of powder."

"Just saying." James nodded toward the door to the tactical room. "This is a good experience. It gets you the feel of a fight without the danger, but the pain is enough to motivate you. Again, if you get shot, go down unless you really want it to hurt."

"You could always turn the shock in my suit off." Alison shrugged.

He snorted. "You have to be a little bit afraid. Now get in there."

Alison rolled her eyes and jogged into the tactical room. Her dad was right. The light coating of magical dust brought the complicated multi-level maze of ramps, hall-ways, blocks, and walls to life before her eyes.

Trey and Shorty jogged her way.

"You ready for this, Alison?" Trey asked.

She nodded. "Just need to murder all my friends, right?"

Trey laughed. "Yeah, that's the spirit. Cap the bastards. Come on, let's go teach a few of the guys a lesson."

He led Alison up a ramp to the second level.

She took several deep breaths as she looked around, the glow of the souls of every man in the room obvious to her. In the confines of the tactical room maze, it was easy to spot even the men who were hiding.

Alison grinned. The game was all about surprise, and she had a major advantage. It almost felt like cheating.

Dad said they *should be more aware of their environment, just like me.*

Trey raised his rifle simulator. "Just keep moving if they close in, and pay attention to when your suit buzzes. This ain't paintball. You hear the shots, but the only way you'll know if they are landing close to you is that buzzing."

The lights flashed a few times to signal the start of the match.

Half the other team jumped out of their cover and opened fire. Alison ducked, her suit buzzing. She waited for it to subside and then followed the energy of one of the enemies running up the ramp—Lachlan, judging by his soul. She stepped behind a wall and waited for him.

Alison squeezed the trigger without hesitation, and Lachlan fell to the ground with a hiss.

"Damn, girl. It's like you can see through walls."

Almost.

Alison's face broke out in a grin. Winning was fun, especially against all the trained bounty hunters. More cries of pain and grunts echoed in the small room. She glanced around. Both her team members and members of the other team were dropping.

Alison ran the opposite way and rushed down a ramp. Her suit buzzed, and she spun and returned fire. The enemy crouched behind a large block, his energy obvious on the edges.

The girl waited, her gun raised, and nailed him in the head when he stood. He yelped and collapsed.

Alison winced. "That looked like it hurt." She wedged herself into a narrow opening underneath one of the ramps and waited, her rifle up.

Two enemies ran right by, and she downed them both. She wiggled out of the opening, laughing. She didn't even need the special earbud the way things were going.

"All that big training and my scrawny little butt is taking you—" Alison yelped as a jolt struck her leg from the side. She burst out laughing and fell to the ground. "It tickles."

Two matches later, Trey grabbed Alison and pulled her aside.

"Staff Sergeant said they're gonna turn the smoke on this time, so visibility's gonna be bad," Trey commented.

Alison shrugged. "Just have to find them and shoot them."

Trey looked back and forth and leaned in to whisper. "Look, I've been watching you. You're good. Better than almost anybody here, and I see you picking off people I didn't even know were there."

She nibbled her lip. "Beginner's luck?"

The bounty hunter smirked. "Ain't no such thing, little girl. I know your dad's been telling you not to use magic, but I figure you slipped a little in this time or something." He held up a hand to cut her off from speaking. "Don't need to know the details. This is a game, not the street. But you go high and just let me know where the other guys are. We take this when it's already two-one, we win."

Alison grinned. "I'll admit I have a few tricks up my sleeve."

Trey raised his rifle simulator. "Then it's time to show

them that James isn't the only Brownstone they should be afraid of."

Alison was happy to get out of the suit. The sweet taste of victory lingered, but so did the BO that came from being trapped in the tactical jumpsuit for three full grueling matches. She finished pulling it off and dropped it into a box near the exit. Her shorts and T-shirt were soaked with sweat.

Several shouts of "Good job, Alison" followed as the men finished removing their jumpsuits and wandered toward the hallway leading to the showers.

Trey waited near the door, his arms crossed, until the rest of the men had departed. James turned the corner and headed toward the pair.

Alison waved. "Hi, Dad."

James smiled. "Hey, kid."

Trey pushed off the wall. "Hey, Alison, you know what the most important part of being a bounty hunter is?"

She shrugged. "Kicking butt?"

"Nah, that's easy. It's noticing shi…stuff. It's how we track guys down, and I noticed some stuff in those matches."

"I thought we already talked about this."

James frowned and crossed his arms.

Trey shook his head. "Nah, the thing is, I was thinking this was all just magic, but then I've been noticing how you move since you've come here. How you look at people—or don't look at people."

"And?" Alison held her breath.

"You blind, aren't you? But I know you can tell when people are coming at you. I figure you're blind, but you make it up with magic somehow. Maybe magic sonar or something like that." Trey grinned.

Alison blinked and looked at James. He gave her a nod.

"I see magical energy and the energy of life, particularly souls. I can also tell when people are lying because of it."

Trey shook his head. "Damn. Now that would be handy. All this makes a lot more sense." He glanced at James. "Why didn't you tell us, big man?"

The bounty hunter shrugged. "She doesn't like people to know, so it's not my business to tell people."

"Fine, then I won't tell the boys. They can figure it out themselves." Trey gave them a little mocking salute and walked away. "Until next time. I fear the day she ain't on my team."

James and Alison chuckled. The bounty hunter's phone buzzed, and he looked at the incoming message.

"Shay's coming to pick you up for knife training and grenade practice."

The teen laughed. "I wonder if I should tell people I practiced with grenades in the summer."

James grunted. "Big deal. You go to a magic school. Grenades are nothing compared to the kind of thing you'll be able to do. Shay's also got a different sort of obstacle course set up at Warehouse One. Just remember what we said about its location."

Alison snorted. "If there's one thing I can do, it's keep a secret."

An hour later, James was on his way across the parking lot to his F-350 when his phone rang. He looked down. Unknown number.

Heather, huh? She knows better than I do about the best way to keep safe.

"Yeah, what's up?" James answered. "Oh, I talked to Mack for you."

"Mack?" replied a soft female voice over the line.

James didn't recognize the voice. It didn't sound anything like Heather.

"Who is this?" the bounty hunter rumbled.

The woman laughed. "Oh, no, no. That's not how this is going to go, James."

He grunted. "Only my friends get to call me James, and I have no fucking idea who you are."

"I'm the woman who has power over you."

James snorted. "Only two women like that on this planet, and you aren't either of them."

"You're going to be doing some things for me, along with giving me money though, soon enough." She chuckled.

"And why would I do that?"

The woman blew out a breath. "Because I have a video of you doing some very, very kinky stuff, and I think the internet would be very interested in it."

James burst out laughing. "Seriously? That's the shit you're gonna try?"

"Did you hear what I said?"

"I don't think you have that shit, but even if you did,

what the fuck ever." James shook his head. "Here's the thing… I wouldn't release the video, for your sake."

The woman snickered. "You think you can threaten me, James?"

"Nah. You're not understanding. I'm not threatening you. I'm just saying if you did something like that, some people I know would track you down. You wouldn't be alive at the end of it, and trust me, I'm not gonna be the one touching you. So, for your own sake, just give up on whatever bullshit blackmail scheme you think you have going."

The woman harrumphed. "This isn't over, James." The woman ended the call.

James heaved a huge sigh. It'd been only a matter of time before something like this happened. Time for some damage control.

He dialed Heather at her last contact number.

"Hey, James," the hacker answered. "I got a call from the cop. Thanks for putting in a good word for me."

"No problem. I've got a job for you."

"Oh?"

James could almost hear the grin over the line.

"Yeah." He frowned. "Some bitch just called me up and tried to blackmail me. Claims she has kinky video of me. Called my phone from an unknown number."

Heather laughed. "And does she have kinky video?"

"I'm not a kinky sort of guy. Kinky is complicated, and I've got enough complicated shit in my life, let alone in the bedroom." James shook his head. "Just track her down before Shay finds out, Peyton finds her, and Shay ends her."

"Aye-aye, James. I'll find your mystery bitch ASAP."

James chuckled. "Thanks." He ended the call.

All the mirth drained from him. The timing was too damn convenient. Someone was threatening to release a kinky video of him right before a court hearing to determine if he could adopt Alison. Coincidence?

Maybe, or maybe someone was trying to sabotage his case.

Find this bitch, Heather. If she's trying to fuck with the adoption, I'll make her pay.

10

The next day, Trey, Royce, and James sat at a table in a conference room. They'd been discussing training over the last several days, and how pleased Royce was with the men's overall progress since the start of the program.

"All that said, it's time for another Mud King match," Royce announced. "It's a good exercise, and teamwork in different contexts only helps."

Trey nodded. "Yeah, it really stuck with the boys, and I think they'd work hard to get their shot at victory."

James furrowed his brow. "I agree, but I think we should change it.

Royce nodded. "Sure. What did you have in mind?"

"Maybe we can do the finals differently."

The DI frowned. "Yeah, to be honest, I don't know how much chance they have with you. They could use some better tactics, but your physical abilities are just way above them. You should be a target, but not an impossible one."

"I wasn't even thinking about that. I was just thinking

that maybe Shay and Alison could be involved. You know, Team Brownstone?" James shrugged.

Trey laughed. "So the other team can get their ass handed to them even easier? I saw Shay on our obstacle course once. The woman moves like gravity's optional for her."

Royce shook his head. "I've got an idea. We can use technology similar to what we use in the tactical training suits. There are vests I can get my hands on. They deliver shocks if three places are touched in the space of one second. I've seen them used in similar types of training before, where they were trying to get people to focus on particular areas of the body."

"With all this shocking going on, we're all gonna end up fucking sterile," Trey muttered.

"It gives more options on how to take out a competitor. It encourages not just brute strength, but also stealth and surprise attacks. It means someone like Alison has a shot at taking out someone, but also a normal man has a shot at taking James out." Royce glanced at the bounty hunter. "The shock will be strong enough to stun someone so they can be more easily pushed."

"Someone, but not necessarily me." James grunted.

"It's not that weak."

"Maybe. I can take a shock or two." He shrugged. "If I can be shot a few times and not go down, I'm not gonna drop from a shock."

Royce chuckled. "Fair enough. It'll at least slow you down. If they're smart, they'll go after you in pairs. The second guy can keep up the shocks after you go down from the first guy's attack.

"Yeah, guess you're right." James grinned, excitement already starting to build. "Talk to Charlyce about getting the order in. This sounds like a good idea."

Shay frowned as Alison ran through the empty shelves she'd set up in Warehouse One. The girl stumbled over a box and scrambled up. She made it a few more feet before the tomb raider nailed her with a small rubber ball. It was enough to sting, but not enough to injure her.

The teen yelped and ducked as Shay picked up a few more from a nearby box and threw them at Alison.

"Keep low," the tomb raider shouted. "You're already small, which means you're a harder target to hit. The less you present, the harder it is."

Alison felt her way around another shelf then darted around the corner just in time to dodge another rubber ball.

The girl reached the end of the shelves and leaned over, panting and rubbing her side.

"That hurt, Aunt Shay," Alison whined.

"That's the point. I don't have those fancy suits like James. Need something to motivate you." Shay nodded, satisfied with what she was seeing. "Plus, you need to look at me more. You might be blind, but you can see enough of a person's energy to at least anticipate their actions. Avoiding attacks is similar to avoiding a tail. You need to be unpredictable, and you need to anticipate what the other person will do."

Alison sighed and stood up. "All this training, though…

I appreciate it, but I don't know if it'll help. I thought it would, but now I'm not so sure. At the end of the day, I still can't see like you can, so even if I can avoid the other person shooting at me, I'm going to trip over a box."

Shay frowned. She'd wanted the girl to appreciate the possible situations and the dangers she might face. James' magical-powder-covered training courses didn't present real-world environments, but the tomb raider might have pushed too far.

She let out a long sigh and walked over to Alison. "This is partially our fault."

"What do you mean?"

Shay shrugged. "James and I *don't* see like you do, so the only thing we can do is train you the ways we know. But you have advantages we don't. He told me how handy your sight was in the tactical room. The same principles apply with a real gun."

Alison snorted. "Doesn't mean anything if I trip and get shot because I'm falling."

"I know. I know." Shay took a deep breath. "I'm looking into magic that can help you see better, so you don't have to worry about using your wish for it. It's going to be a while, though. I can't honestly say when it'll be ready."

The teen nodded. "I don't even know what to say. I've never thought much about using an artifact to help with my sight."

Shay shrugged. "My day job is finding artifacts. I wish I could find one to really help you. Maybe give you complete normal vision."

Alison shook her head. "But I don't want that."

"You don't want to see normally?"

"No." The girl smiled. "I like being able to see the truth of people's souls. Without it, I wouldn't have known how beautiful your soul is, or Dad's."

Shay snorted. "You need to get those eyes checked if you think my soul is beautiful."

"Doing bad things doesn't mean you have a bad soul." Alison pulled Shay into an embrace. "I can see the pain in both you and Dad. I wish I could help you let it go, but I know you're both good people because you both have helped me and care about me."

Shay blinked away a few rogue tears and patted Alison on the head before pulling out of the embrace.

Damn it. This girl is getting to me. I love her and James. I know that makes me soft, but I don't give a shit.

She cleared her throat. "Just because you said all that doesn't mean I'm going to throw softer during the next round of training." The tomb raider marched over to the shelves. "The great thing about these things is that they are easy to move around. Get ready for round two."

Alison groaned.

Yev sat in the comfortable seat in front of the senator's desk and folded his hands. "We appreciate your efforts in this matter so far, Senator. I've been informed that other Oriceran groups appreciate your efforts as well."

The human gave him a quick nod. "From what I've been told, there's plenty of stuff in the public record that Brownstone has done. It'll be pretty easy to convince a family court judge to deny the adoption. The real problem comes after that."

"Oh?"

The senator nodded. "We might not get so lucky next time. What if someone else wants to adopt her? We can't make a good case for why *no one* can adopt her, only him. Not everyone has a background like James Brownstone's. From what you told me, this girl needs to go back to Oriceran."

Yev sighed. "Please forgive me for the indelicacy of this suggestion, but if it comes down to that, we're prepared to leak some of the seedier details of her family life, including the death of her father and how her mother is still missing. It's my understanding that human families aren't as interested in adopting older children anyway."

"That sounds about right." The senator rubbed his chin. "You're pretty savvy for an elf. Come to think of it, we can use some of that strategy now."

"You want us to go after the girl?"

The senator shook his head. "No. We can make this easier if we provoke Brownstone. He's already got a suspicious connection to this thing. He killed the father."

Yev shrugged. "The police say it was in self-defense, and that the father was a criminal."

"Who cares? If we push that in the press, he'll look like a trigger-happy madman who is trying to snatch the daughter of the man he murdered. Get a few tabloid sites to run with that angle, and it'll piss Brownstone off. If he makes a spectacle in public, this case will be over before he even steps into the courtroom. I've been pushing my contacts to get negative statements about him from the local police, but no one seems to want to play ball."

Yev sighed. "He's earned many allies. I don't wish to destroy him, but what we're doing here is for the good of both planets. No one man's honor is worth war. The people of both Earth and Oriceran understand that. We've learned that lesson through blood, pain, and suffering."

The senator nodded. "Not saying I disagree, but the more we talk about this, the more I worry about how Brownstone will react when the judge rules against him."

"It's my understanding that James Brownstone is very respectful of human authority. Your difficulty in getting the local police to turn against him is proof of that. It means he's been forthright and honorable in his dealings with them."

"He's respectful of authority when it's paying him money to catch criminals." The senator frowned. "How much is he going to like his government when it gets in the way of his adoption? And what if he gets wind the Oricerans were involved in this? What if he comes after us?"

Yev laughed. "Comes after us? What, the entire state of California? As for Oriceran, that's even more absurd. What is Brownstone going to do, attack an entire planet?"

The senator shrugged. "He might blame the Light Elves."

"Oh, that's still an entire race. James Brownstone is an impressive man, I'll grant you that, but he's neither stupid enough nor powerful enough to take on an entire Oriceran race. He's hardly the first powerful individual Light Elves have faced."

"You sound so sure." The senator leaned back in his chair and crossed his arms. "He took on those Drow. *They* were pretty damned tough."

Yev waved a hand dismissively. "He didn't take on the Drow *race*. He took on a handful of Drow." He sighed. "I'm not saying we shouldn't be surreptitious in our dealings in this matter, but you can't honestly believe that James Brownstone is a legitimate threat to your government or the Light Elves."

The senator chuckled. "You're right. I'm just letting the hype get to me." He nodded. "If he comes after me it won't just be AET taking him down; it'll be the National Guard." His smile disappeared. "And if he comes after you, he's going to have to deal with the power of magic. I've seen the kind of things that can be pulled off when you go all out."

"Exactly." Yev smiled. "He'll slink away, defeated, and the half-Drow girl will welcome a respite from her pain. A trip to Oriceran might be just the thing."

"You sound pretty confident."

"That comes with the centuries. Soon, this whole problem will go away, and we'll laugh about having ever worried about James Brownstone."

11

James chomped on his rib, which was smothered in one of his more North Carolina-flavored experimental sauces. The balance of the pepper and vinegar was excellent.

He frowned. The sauce was good, but it wasn't great. They weren't going to win competitions with merely good sauce.

Needs a touch of something. Not sure yet. Shit, need to start practicing more. The guys are gonna expect me to be the leader in this. Don't want to look like a fucking chump when it comes to barbeque.

Alison smirked, then bit into one of her ribs with a mocking glint in her eye.

What? Does she not like my sauce either? She never cared that much before.

Enough ribs and brisket to feed a small army lay on two large trays in the center of James' dining room table. The girl sat on one side, James and Shay the other. Everything about it was relaxed, and they resembled a normal family eating a delicious meal.

Sure, one participant was a half-Drow girl attending a government magic school, another a tomb raider and former killer, and the last an alien bounty hunter, but their mutual love was as normal and warm as any three people's.

Is this what it means to be normal? I like this. I didn't even know I needed this for so long but damned if I don't love it. But what's up with that shit-eating grin? Is this more teenage shit? Or do I have something on my face?

James furrowed his brow. "Something funny, Alison? Or were you just thinking about that mall training thing and how you got one over on Shay."

Shay snorted and eyed Alison. "Don't get too cocky, kid. Two out of ten is a good start, but it's not exactly a passing score."

The girl shook her head. "Nothing like that. I had always wondered how long it'd take before we had our first home-cooked barbeque meal together. It took a lot longer than I would have bet."

"Nothing wrong with a little barbeque." James shrugged.

"Not saying that. If anything, it makes me feel more relaxed. It's just so…James Brownstone. I truly know I'm home now." Alison laughed, the sound light, airy, and free.

James grunted. If anything, barbeque might be a more fundamental part of him than the amulet. Maybe he came from the Planet of Pit Masters.

The weight of Alison's use of "home" filled him with even more warmth. He'd visited her several times, but she'd been away for a long time. He hadn't been sure whether she'd started thinking of the school as her real home.

"Guess we'll be having a lot of barbeque over the summer," James rumbled.

Shay snickered. "Yeah, use any excuse for that. Convenient. I'm sure we would have had less barbeque if she'd said she hated it."

"I don't know. Maybe."

Shay rolled her eyes and turned to Alison. "Forget barbeque. You've completed your first year at magic school, so how does that feel? It's not exactly something the average teen girl gets to experience, even these days. I don't know if that's ever gonna be the case."

Alison shrugged. "I feel a lot better than I did at the start. I have much better control of my magic now, and you know how much I was worried about that when I started. It might not be home when I'm there, but I'm comfortable there. Every day I get a little stronger, even if it's not obstacle-course strong. And I have friends."

"Friends are good," James rumbled. "Even *I* have a few nowadays. It's weird."

Shay held up a rib and pointed at Alison with it. "Friends are good to have, especially if they'll help you bury a body."

Alison burst out laughing. "Aunt Shay, seriously? That's what you think friends are good for?"

The tomb raider winked. "Just saying. A good friend will help you move, but a real friend will help you move a body."

The teen broke into even louder laughter.

It took a good ten seconds before Alison regained

control. She wiped away a few laughter tears.

"Plus, I've learned so much about the history of Oriceran, including the history of the Drow, but I have to admit it's weird reading about them. I…don't know if I'll end up like them."

James shrugged. "Just because you're half-Drow doesn't mean you have to do what they do."

"I know. It's just I grew up in a country that gets a new president every four to eight years. Laena has ruled the Drow for centuries."

"Laena?" James grunted, not having known the name of the woman sending people after him.

"Yes. She's the current Drow queen. Anyway, the point is that I still have so much to learn. So many different races, and so many thousands of years. It's hard to take in, but I feel like I'm getting closer to the truth, and it makes my head spin."

"Good." Shay gave her a warm smile. "History's important." She chuckled. "The fact that we didn't know our true history on Earth until recently means we've misunderstood things, and made more than a few mistakes because of it. You've grown up your entire life knowing more of the truth than a lot of adults."

James put down his latest rib, which had been stripped of meat in half a minute. "And you've been okay there at the school? No problems with bullies or anything? I can always come by for a little one-on-one chat session with any bullies."

Alison gave him a sly smile that suggested she was holding something back. "I'm doing fine, Dad. It's not like anyone wants to mess with the daughter of the great James

Brownstone." She rolled her eyes. "If anything, you coming by more might scare too many people away."

"Good."

"Good?"

The bounty hunter decided to go for some brisket this time. "That's the power of a reputation. You use mine until you develop your own."

"Sure, if you say so."

Again, something about Alison's smile made him feel like there was stuff he didn't know.

Should I press her on it? Nah. My reputation is following her around, and both Shay and Alison have beat it into my head that I need to give her some independence. She'll be fine, especially after we finish training her this summer.

James cleared his throat. "Seems like you've gotten used to training with both Shay and me. You're doing better than I thought you would."

Alison laughed. "Not like I had a choice, but, sure, I get it. And the tactical room is fun, especially when the guys yelp." She grinned. "And also because I can see their energy so easily, and most of them haven't figured it out."

Shay took a sip of her drink, a bottle of beer, and nodded. "Good. Here's a nice lesson to absorb: Never give up unnecessary information, even to your friends."

James shrugged. "It took *me* a while to figure out. You don't exactly move like a normal blind person." He set his food down. "Hey, I had something I needed to ask you both before, and now is as good a time as any."

The two women in his life stared at him expectantly.

"We're doing that mud pit challenge stuff again at the Brownstone Agency, and they are gonna be changing the rules a little bit. Royce is gonna get us vests so you can take people out just by touching them. It'll be more tactical and crap that way, instead of just a contest of strength. Because I just win too easily when it's about nothing but strength."

Shay and Alison both nodded.

James grunted then continued, "So anyway, the last round was the winning team against me, but I think this time it should be the winning team against Team Brownstone." He pointed to Alison and Shay in turn. "And that means you two on my team."

Shay shrugged. "Sure? Why the hell not? Just don't blame me if I hurt any of your guys' feelings. I wonder if a lot of them can handle getting their ass kicked by a woman."

The bounty hunter chuckled. "I think most of them are already afraid of you."

"Good. That means they aren't idiots."

James turned to Alison. "And you? It'll be easy to keep track of people since it'll just be Shay and me on your team."

Alison sighed. "You want me to roll around in mud?"

"Not roll around, just push or trip other people. Or touch their vests to shock them."

"Shock them? Your agency is so twisted."

"Got to have some way to even things out."

Alison grinned. "Fine, Dad. I'll do it for you. I can't wait to go back to school and tell all my friends how I spent the first part of my summer running obstacle courses and rolling around in mud while they were probably off vacationing on tropical islands and swimming."

All three laughed.

James' laugh drifted into silence as a warm smile took over his face.

Eating as a family, taking down bounty hunters in a mud pit as a family. That was what it meant to be a Brownstone.

The next morning, James was thumbing through a list of county barbeque competitions when his phone rang. It was his lawyer.

The bounty hunter frowned. Even though his lawyer might be calling to deliver good news, he doubted it.

"Yeah," he answered in a rumble.

"I take it you haven't been reading or watching any news this morning, have you?" the lawyer asked.

James grunted. "I don't pay that much attention to the news in general unless it's barbeque shit or bounties. What difference does it make if I know what the fuck is going on?"

The lawyer sighed. "I guess that's a good thing, but as your attorney, I still have a duty to advise you about this matter."

"What matter?"

"The media is suddenly very interested in this adoption case, and they're really playing up your violent background and how you were even responsible for killing Walt Anderson." The attorney clucked his tongue. "The Brownstone-as-Thug meme will be the main thrust of the government's case against you."

James' hand tightened around his phone. A little more

pressure and the glass would crack. "The LAPD didn't have a problem with that, and the guy was a scumbag. I'm not in fucking prison, so that should mean something."

"The court of public opinion can be a nasty thing." The lawyer let out another long sigh. "We're not talking about criminal culpability here, though. We're talking about a family court judge deciding whether you'll be a good guardian for an orphaned girl."

The bounty hunter gritted his teeth. "So what are you saying?"

Hope crept into the lawyer's voice. "Look, right now, I think it's not a big deal. We both knew something like this might be coming, and we've got official statements of character coming in from police and city officials in LA, Las Vegas, Detroit, and even Tokyo. Father McCartney is working on a statement, and he's getting his bishop to write one, talking about how your financial support has been critical to keeping that orphanage open. I just got off the phone before calling you with a government official from Mexico who wants to write a statement on your behalf. Most of these people have also agreed to testify on your behalf."

James gritted his teeth and took a deep breath. "So this news stuff is just bullshit, right?"

The lawyer swallowed, the sound audible even over the phone. "I called to warn you that this is just the beginning. They are going to do a full court press, James. I don't even think this is about poisoning public opinion. The judge is fair, and he'll take into account every character statement and other evidence we submit."

"Then what the hell is this about?"

The lawyer paused for a few seconds before responding. "I think they are trying to get you to react. A video of you punching a reporter would be enough to doom your adoption, especially given their general thug strategy."

James grunted. "Why does everyone assume I'll get violent?"

The lawyer didn't respond.

I only kick the asses of people who really have it coming. I spent my life cleaning up trash, and now some assholes want to say that means I shouldn't get to adopt Alison?

"I'm not a fucking thug."

The lawyer yelped. "Calm down, James. It's important that you remain very calm over the next few weeks. Also, you need to not react even when you're not the target."

"What do you mean when I'm not the target?"

A few beats of silence ticked by. "The main media sources will generally leave Alison out of this, but the tabloids are going to play up her half-Oriceran nature. I've already seen some of that sort of thing. It's nasty, to be honest, and unfair to the girl. Racism or speciesism, whatever you want to call it. Quite frankly, I'm surprised the news is already everywhere. I think someone leaked her heritage information to the press."

James growled. "They should leave her out of this. If I get my hands—"

"Restraint, James. They want you to react. Ignore them. If you can keep yourself under control, it doesn't matter what the press says, tabloid or not."

"I'm fine," the bounty hunter responded, his voice still low and full of menace. "I just have to put up with a bunch of fuckers calling me a piece of shit for a few months, no big deal. I can do this." He blew out a breath and resisted the urge to smash his phone against the wall.

Those fuckers. They better hope Shay or me never meet them in a dark alley.

The lawyer let out a nervous chuckle. "Well, at least in regards to how long you have to control yourself, I have some good news."

"Good news?" James loosened the tight group he had on his phone.

"That was the other main reason I called you. I filed a motion for an expedited hearing. It was a long shot, but they've agreed to it."

James frowned. "Meaning what?"

"You won't have to put up with the character assassinations for months, only a week. I'm honestly surprised they accepted the motion, but I think that no one wants such a high-profile case lingering around making the government look bad. I don't know who is involved in spreading the negative media stories about you and Alison, but there's a lot of online pushback against the fact that the government's even fighting this adoption." The lawyer laughed. "Multiple petitions coming in from your fans all over the world, along with both human and Oriceran groups advocating for assimilation and coexistence. A few have filed some amicus briefs on your behalf."

"Will any of that shit help?"

"Not sure, but at a minimum, it'll keep the state's lawyers on the straight and narrow. Any appearance of impropriety on their part will be blasted around the world via the net in an hour."

James nodded. At least *something* was working to their

advantage.

As the lawyer explained a few more details, the bounty hunter's thoughts drifted to other plans. No matter what, he wouldn't let anyone take Alison. He had a duty to protect the girl and not only that, he loved her like he'd been her father his entire life.

Don't worry, kid. I won't let them take you, no matter what I have to do.

Maria trudged into the Black Sun with a deep frown on her face. She moved through the crowd, the crowd of men parting instinctively as she made her way to the bar. No one wanted to be on AET's radar.

Tyler set a beer down in front of her before she'd sat on her stool. "You look pissed. Not that it's a new look for you, but just saying."

The cop gulped some beer before answering. "I've just been looking into why the state's pushing back against Brownstone's adoption. Getting a lot of suspicious stonewalling. I was wondering if you could look into some of that. I know government snooping isn't your normal wheelhouse, but something smells here, so I thought you might be able to find shit that I can't." She smirked. "Besides, most politicians are criminals, and criminals are your thing."

The bartender shrugged. "When I asked you about Brownstone earlier, I was curious more than anything. It's not like we have to help him."

"Don't we?" Maria quirked a brow.

Tyler blinked. "Why would we? This isn't some crazy bounty coming after him. This is the government we're talking about."

"Maybe *you* don't give a shit, but it's my job."

"How is it your job? I mean, the girl seems cool enough and all, but how is helping Brownstone by poking the government your job?" Tyler stared at her, confusion written all over his face.

Maria took another long drag of her beer. "My job is to make the city safe, right?"

"Yeah, but that doesn't have fuck-all to do with an adoption."

She shook her head. "Wrong. One of the reasons this city is safe is because of Brownstone. I bet if Brownstone had been in town when Tessa Vansant showed up, there wouldn't have been a farmers market massacre. So, anyone fucking with Brownstone is fucking with the safety of the city." She pointed her beer bottle at Tyler. "So, yeah, my job."

"Okay, fair enough." Tyler shrugged. "But that doesn't make it *my* job. I'm not a cop."

Maria smirked. "It's in your best interests that this city not be turned into a crater."

"Still…"

She leaned forward. "And if you want that date Friday night, you're going to help me."

Tyler blinked. "What date?"

Maria winked. "Going to play along, or what?"

"Okay, okay." The bartender shrugged. "I'll sniff around, but I'm not guaranteeing anything."

"That's all I ask."

James eyed Shay's obstacle as Alison moved toward it in Shay's training course in Warehouse One. He was still unsure whether letting the teen move around the tomb raider's course was a good idea, even just part of it.

"It's okay." Shay laughed. It was as if she could read his mind. "She won't be able to do them all, but I've got them coated with the powder, so she can at least try some of them. Plus, I put down mats, so it's way safer than when I do it."

"I'm doing fine, Dad," Alison called. "Just part of doing the Tomb Raider Dance."

Peyton leaned toward Shay and James. "Isn't she, like, you know, blind?" he whispered. "That was the excuse you used for bringing her to the warehouse—that she wouldn't exactly be able to give people directions."

Shay snorted. "Not like she'd ever betray me anyway."

James shrugged. "She can see some. I don't know. Enough? Like Shay said, we've got the shit set up so she can see what she needs to do the obstacles. Anyway, she's fine. What we need to do is figure out this adoption stuff."

The bounty hunter nodded toward a corner, and the three walked that way so they could discuss things more privately.

Peyton looked at James and Shay. "So, I've been trying to poke around, but carefully, so no one gets suspicious and comes knocking on your door."

James nodded. "I wonder if I should have Heather start looking, too."

"I've got this." The hacker frowned at James.

Shay rolled her eyes. "Put your dick back in your pants, Peyton. Anyone and anything that can help is on the table. This is about making sure the government doesn't take Alison away, not your male ego."

Peyton grimaced. "Sorry."

"No problem." James grunted. "Probably wouldn't help much anyway since she's trying to get ready to move. Turn up anything?"

"Nothing super-suspicious. All the court documents and records I can find seem normal. The only thing that is weird is how they knew about a lot of the stuff people are complaining about now before. It's in their files." Peyton shrugged. "The School of Necessary Magic sent documents to the government in Virginia and California when she first enrolled that discussed her being half-Oriceran, so it's not like they just realized it. It's been a matter of public record for a while if you knew what to look for."

James grunted. He hadn't thought a lot about the state complaining about that aspect of things. He'd assumed the minute he sent her to a government magic school that she'd lost her privacy, but as Peyton suggested, he'd also assumed that if there were going to be any trouble, it would have been then.

The bounty hunter glanced at Shay before looking back at Peyton. "Why the fuck do they suddenly care then?"

"Your guess is as good as mine. I might have to poke deeper into some of the state systems. Really dig deep."

Shay shook her head. "Don't know if that's a great idea." She held up a hand to cut him off before he could start to bitch. "Look, we fuck anything up, it's gonna give them ammunition. So, do what you need to, but tread really fucking lightly. Until and unless we have proof of some criminal asshole being involved in all this, we can't go kicking in doors like we might on a normal job. For now, just have to keep a low profile and do what the fucking lawyer tells us to."

James nodded. He didn't like the idea of sitting around doing nothing, but it was like Shay said. His normal skills just didn't serve him well in an adoption battle with the state of California. Blowing up the courthouse or slaughtering the government lawyers would earn him a ticket to an ultra-max, not Alison.

"Oof!" Alison yelled from across the room.

James' head snapped that way. She'd fallen from the wall. His stomach tightened.

Damn it.

Peyton scrubbed a hand over his face. "Having a blind girl climb a wall…" He sighed. "Just saying."

Alison stood and rolled her eyes. "Could have died there. Okay, attempt number two." She leapt onto the climbing wall. "Time for my revenge, wall."

A mix of pride and terror swirled in James.

Shay smiled at him. "Congratulations."

"For what?"

"You're proving you can change a little and not be overprotective. I figured you'd freak and rush over there to help her the second she started to struggle."

"*Started* to struggle?" James stared at her, confused. "She just fell."

"Yeah. It's not like she suddenly fell off. Didn't you see that her feet were in the wrong position before that?"

The bounty hunter shook his head and shrugged. "I figured it's your place and you care, so you were watching her."

Shay bit her lip, her face reddening. "You were relying on me?"

"Yeah, why the fuck wouldn't I? You love her, too. That's not some big fucking mystery."

The tomb raider stared down at the floor, her face turning scarlet.

Peyton grinned and opened his mouth, but shut it when James gave him a death glare. This wasn't a time for him to poke at his boss.

Might not always know what the fuck is going on, but don't want anyone going at Shay for giving a shit about Alison.

The hacker cleared his throat. "I have to…uh…go to the bathroom. I'll be right back." He spun on his heel and hurried around the corner, paler than before.

Shay looked up. "You're pretty smart for a walking brick sometimes." She looked into James' eyes, a soft smile on her face. "A damned sexy brick, but still."

James chuckled. "I have my moments."

The tomb raider stepped toward him and wrapped her arms around his waist. "You're a good man, James Brownstone. Don't ever forget that. Just because the government is being a dick doesn't mean shit."

She bit her lip again, her gaze roving his body. She ran her hands along his thick biceps.

"Geeze," Alison yelled from the other side of the room. "Get a room, you two."

Shay jerked away from James and shot a glare toward the climbing wall. "I'm going to have to kill you."

Alison waved from the wall. "You won't. You love me too much." She continued up the wall.

James cleared his throat. "Just both of you remember about the Mud King challenge."

Shay snorted. "Whatever. The Mud Queens will put an end to that title."

James stepped into the armory at the Brownstone Building. Trey, Shorty, Max, and Lachlan stood in front of the equipment racks and shelves. They were strapping on their tactical harnesses, vests, and gear.

Shorty slipped a pistol into a holster. "Brownstone Building sounds like boring shit."

Trey nodded toward Alison and James, and the other bounty hunter grimaced.

The teen snickered.

"Got a better suggestion?" James rumbled.

Shorty squared his shoulders and lifted his head. "Yeah,

I do. We get trained by a Marine. Why don't we think more like them?"

"Meaning?"

Shorty grinned. "I think we should call this place 'Camp Brownstone.'"

The other men present, even Trey, nodded their agreement. A few "Hell yeahs" came out.

James shrugged. He didn't really give a shit, but the men seemed into it. "Camp Brownstone it is."

Trey walked over to him. "What's up, big man? We were about to hit a bounty. Not a big deal, just a level two. Probably could take him by myself, but we're trying to reinforce the team thing."

"Yeah, I know. That's why I came." James nodded toward Alison. "And brought her."

"Not following you." Trey frowned.

James turned to Alison. "Go get your gear on. No gun, though."

Trey blinked. "You want her to come along?"

James nodded. "She's not gonna be a bounty hunter, but she asked me the other night, and it's good experience. I'm coming too to keep an eye on her, but I'm gonna hang back and just let you guys do your thing."

Trey laughed. "Mr. Brownstone himself, his magical daughter, and four guys for a level two. Talk about overkill. The guy's not even that tough, just embezzlement. There's an easy pick-up we can grab too, a level one. Another petty criminal."

Alison had made her way to where her vest was hanging, drawn by the small enchantment James had arranged to make her vest and tactical harness visible to her.

James frowned at a sudden realization. Anyone who could detect magic would be able to pick her out, even if she were hiding.

Shit. Did I fuck up?

He pushed the thought from his head. Alison wasn't going to be a bounty hunter, and her coming along was just about her experiencing a little more of the world and getting to see the kind of work he did up close.

Trey was right. A full crew plus James would be more than enough to capture any bounties and still protect Alison.

The bounty hunter surveyed his men. It wasn't all that long ago that they were directionless gangbangers, but now every single one, even Lachlan, was an experienced bounty hunter. Disciplined. Good under pressure.

James allowed himself a smile. Royce and Trey had done the hard work of shaping the gang members into bounty hunters, but that didn't mean the bounty hunter wouldn't let himself take a little pride in the men.

"Let's go, Team Brownstone," James rumbled. "We have some ass to kick."

<hr>

Trey adjusted his tie. The thinner vest could be worn comfortably under his suit, even if it gave him a bulky, almost Isaiah-like frame, but there were some sacrifices a man had to be prepared to suffer for proper style.

Ain't gonna ever look like a fucking lame-ass bitch on the job.

He knocked on the door and waited with a smile. Alison and James were in James' F-350, watching from across the road. The rest of the team had driven to the scene in Trey's F-350.

Should make every one of those motherfuckers buy a classic truck. Another Brownstone Agency signature. People will learn to fear the fucking Ford.

A sweaty man in glasses opened the door. "C-can I help you?"

Trey offered him a polite smile. With the anxious bounties, sometimes a little Smooth Trey could go a long way.

"Good afternoon, sir. You're Cameron Booth, correct?"

The man quickly nodded. "What about it? Who are you?"

The bounty hunter sighed. "You seem like a nice guy, Cameron, which is why it's unfortunate that some bad, bad men are on their way for you right now."

"B-bad men?" Cameron's knees started shaking.

"Yeah. You see, I'm Trey Garfield. I work with the Brownstone Agency."

He waited for that to sink in.

"A-as in James Brownstone?"

"Yep. The big man himself. Scourge of Harriken. Granite Ghost. Etcetera, etcetera." Trey waved. "Anyway, the point is, at the Brownstone Agency, we pride ourselves on professionalism. When a man surrenders to us, there doesn't need to be a bunch of violence and unnecessary pain." He clucked his tongue. "But some sons of bitches… Well, they call themselves bounty hunters, but really they aren't much more than thugs, you know what I'm saying?" He shrugged.

Cameron spun around. Trey grabbed for his gun, but he stopped a second later. The bounty wasn't running or going for a weapon. He'd turned around and placed his wrists together behind his back.

The man was shaking even more than before. "Please, Mr. Garfield. I can't take pain. I'll admit it. I'm a wimp. I wish I'd never gotten involved in selling that dust. Just… arrest me before someone nasty comes."

Trey chuckled and fished out his handcuffs. He slapped them on Cameron. "Just to be clear, Mr. Booth, I'm not arresting you. I'm not a cop, I'm a bounty hunter. I'm gonna take you with me to a police station for processing. You keep being polite like this, we aren't gonna have a problem." He turned the man and pushed him forward. "Thank you for your cooperation."

"T-thanks, Mr. Garfield, for not hurting me."

"Just gonna take you to that truck over there." Trey forced down a laugh. This had been his easiest bounty in a long time.

Alison rolled down her window across the street and started clapping.

Trey offered her a little bow.

Cameron's eyes widened, and he gasped. "T-that's h-him. Brownstone!"

"Oh, don't get your panties in a twist, Booth. I've already got you. You don't have to worry about what it feels like to get taken down by James Brownstone."

***

Trey glanced over his shoulder, his heart pounding. He wasn't all that worried about the bounty, but he didn't like the fact that Alison was out of the truck this time. She'd told him how excited she'd been when he opened the door, but she wanted to be "where the action was" on the next bounty.

Maybe I shouldn't care if her dad doesn't. Fuck, maybe she's as tough as the big man. Being able to run an obstacle course ain't the same thing as being powerful. She's got magic and shit, after all. Maybe he told her not to blow us up with her fireballs and shit.

Trey shook his head and took a deep, cleansing breath. James was there. If it came down to it, he'd make sure Alison was okay.

The four bounty hunters, trailed by James and Alison, moved down the street leading to the townhome that was serving as a safehouse. Their informants had told them the bounty was staying there for at least another day.

Trey nodded toward the house. "Just a reminder of the plan, boys. Shorty's gonna throw open the door, and I flashbang. Then we go in there and secure everyone. Lachlan and Max, you check the back. Should be easy. This guy ain't personally tough, just stole a lot of money and got away."

The door to the townhouse opened when they were still a good thirty yards out.

Lachlan frowned and pointed. "Who the hell is that? That's not our guy."

Trey glanced over his shoulder at James. His boss gave him a nod and stopped. He held up an arm to stop Alison. The girl frowned but said nothing.

Trey and the other three men advanced toward the townhouse. As they moved closer, they realized their new friend was a Light Elf in a black suit who was standing there with his arms crossed, smirking.

The elf uncrossed his arms. "Can I help you, gentlemen?"

Trey looked him up and down. "Nice suit. Armani?"

"Yes, and thanks." The elf sighed. "I'm guessing that you're here about the bounty." He sucked in a breath. "I'll tell you what I told the last few guys. It's better to turn around right now. Not going to try to kill you, but accidents happen, and I hate killing guys in suits. I love human fashion, you see."

Lachlan, Shorty, and Max had their weapons out in the blink of an eye. Trey, still in the lead, kept his hands down. There was still a chance to de-escalate the situation.

Trey shook his head. "We ain't got no beef with you, man."

The elf shrugged. "Oh, but the problem is the gentleman inside. I have a certain financial relationship with him, which means I'm obliged to make sure he doesn't go anywhere until he's paid me certain monies he owes me."

A few melodic notes escaped the elf's mouth, and a shimmering field appeared in front of him.

Trey removed his gun and sighed. "Fucking magic. Always obnoxious."

"Trust me. You can't win against me, not with your weapons."

Alison snorted. "I'll handle this."

"What the…" Trey glanced behind him. Alison was no longer behind James but was instead walking toward the elf.

He looked at James again, and his boss offered another slight nod.

The girl moved to Trey's side and crossed her arms. "I can see your fear, you know. Nice bluff."

The elf's lip curled up in a sneer. "Is that supposed to impress, little…" He frowned and looked the teen up and down. "Who are you? Your magic is…"

"Just someone Laena has an extreme interest in." Alison held up her hand, and a purple flame erupted above her palm. "You just need to ask yourself two questions. First, is it worth it to earn the wrath of the Drow to protect some human embezzler? Second, can you spend that money if you're dead?"

"You're claiming you're a Drow? Impossible. No Drow would work with petty humans like this."

Alison fluffed the back of her hair with her hand. "Are you so sure?"

The elf stared her down for a long moment before he broke and ran the opposite way, his shield moving with him.

Shorty, Lachlan, and Max rushed forward but stopped at Trey's raised arm.

"He ain't the bounty." Trey nodded toward the townhouse. "The bounty's in there. Just go get the asshole. He thought he had a big elf to help him. Now he ain't got nothing."

The three ran into the townhouse, the door still open.

Trey glanced at Alison. "I don't know half of what you were talking about, but are you telling me that you've got some sort of badass Oriceran reputation that scares people from there just as bad as your dad's reputation scares people from Earth?"

Alison laughed and shrugged. "I just happen to be related to a few people, is all."

The bounty hunter chuckled and shook his head. "You Brownstones."

S hay crossed her arms and frowned as she surveyed the viscous brown sludge filling the competition pit at Camp Brownstone. Her mouth curled in a disgusted sneer.

James snorted. "Why are you acting so surprised? It's not like you've never seen this thing before."

"I don't know. I guess it was just a lot funnier when I thought about your guys being in it, instead of me."

Alison laughed.

James grunted. "You get dirty all the time on your job."

Shay rolled her eyes. "Yes, and I get paid a lot of money for that. Whatever. You owe me for this, and you better not complain later when I'm coated in mud."

James chuckled as he strode forward and nodded at Royce, who was standing in front of the gathered men with his arms crossed.

"Listen up," Royce shouted. "You already had a little mud pit fun between two teams the other day after your bounties, but now it's time for something different." He pointed at James, and then at Alison and Shay. "Like I told you, this time it's going to be all of you versus the Brownstone Family. James, Shay, and Alison."

Shay rolled her eyes. "Hey! I'm not a Brownstone."

Alison smiled. "Yet."

"Fine…yet."

Royce waited for the girls to finish before turning back to the gathered men. "Any questions or concerns? Ask now. Not stopping things because you were too dumb to ask ahead of time. Part of the battle is preparing for it."

Lachlan frowned. "Rules all the same?"

The staff sergeant shook his head. "Good question. No, even with the larger team, James is more than enough to handle all of you, and now we're adding his girlfriend and his magical kid. You wouldn't stand a chance, so we're going to do this differently in the slim hope that you can defeat him."

The men all exchanged glances and murmurs. A few looked desperate, but many others were excited.

Royce pointed to several boxes stacked near the door to the building. "Several of you asked me about those earlier, and I told you to wait, that you'd know when it was time." He grinned. "It's now the damned time. The boxes contain special electronic harnesses. They have panels on them. They're conductive and pressure-sensitive, and they work even with a lot of mud on them. Touch all three within a second, and the man or woman wearing it gets a big shock, more than enough to take the average man down. Then it's easier to push him or her past the line."

Trey snorted. "Average man. What about Mr. Brownstone?"

The staff sergeant shrugged. "It'll slow him down at

least. At least with these vests, you stand a chance. Hey, don't worry too much. David *did* beat Goliath."

Half the men laughed. The other half groaned.

Royce headed over to the boxes. "Let's get this crap on so we can see what you're all made of."

Everyone marched over to the boxes to grab a harness.

Royce fished out a smaller one and handed it to Shay. "These might be smaller, but this shit hurts. James made it very clear that I'm not supposed to hold back for either you or the girl."

Shay snorted. "Trust me, I've had a lot worse. I might even let them have a free touch just to see what it feels like."

"Your funeral."

She scratched her cheek. "You know what? I might as well try it out now to see what it feels like."

"Wait, are you ser—"

The tomb raider slapped her hand on the three panels in rapid succession. They were spread out with two on the front, one on the left, one on the right, and the final panel in the back. It was obvious that the participants would need teamwork in most situations to activate the vest of anyone trying to seriously dodge, or they would have to hope for simple arrogance on the part of their target.

The tomb raider gritted her teeth and shook as the vest discharged, pain shooting through her body and out to her limbs. She collapsed to her hands and knees, her breathing ragged and her body twitching for a few more seconds.

Shay took several deep breaths, her muscles still aching from the discharge. Royce's harnesses definitely weren't for casual games on the weekend.

A chorus of impressed gasps and yells filled the area.

Trey winced. "Oh, damn. You shocked yourself? That's the most gangster shit I've ever seen."

"Okay. I admit that really, really fucking hurt." Shay stumbled back up, still swaying a bit. "So you go out of the pit, or you feel that. It's gonna knock you on your ass for sure." She cracked her knuckles and blew out a breath. "Oh, Mama is going to have some fun now. Squealing pigs in mud, coming *up*."

The gathered men exchanged glances, fear creeping into their faces.

The Marine looked at James as the bounty hunter finished strapping on his large harness, a question in his eyes. He was probably wondering what kind of woman James was dating.

James shrugged. *If you only knew the half of it, Royce.*

The trainer's expression softened, and then he nodded to Alison. It was obvious he was still uncomfortable with the idea of the girl being shocked.

"If Alison can do the tactical room, she can do this," James rumbled.

Royce nodded and offered Alison a harness. She smiled and started strapping it on.

No hesitation. She went from whining about having to exercise to jumping at the chance to do this muddy shit with electronic shocks. She's a lot tougher than I ever realized.

After a few minutes, both teams were ready and marched to their respective sides of the pit.

James moved his neck back and forth and grunted. "Lot of guys means a lot of targets. This is gonna be easy."

Shorty raised his hand to flip him off but lowered it at

the sight of Alison. "Just means more people to take your butts down, big man. Hate to embarrass you in front of your woman and your kid, but I got to do what I go to do, you know what I'm saying?"

Shay's gaze flitted from man to man. She had a smirk on her face. Shorty's smile faded, and he frowned. Several of the men took a step back.

She's just trying to intimidate you. Don't be such pussies.

James grunted at the thought and reconsidered his judgment. Considering what he'd seen from Shay in the past, a little fear was probably healthier and safer. Being afraid of Shay meant they could sense when someone was more dangerous than them, a good skill for any bounty hunter to have.

Royce cleared his throat. "If the Brownstone Family doesn't mind, I suggest we do best two out of three. Sometimes it takes a little while to figure things out."

James shrugged. "Sounds good to me."

Alison and Shay both nodded their agreement, bloodlust, or mudlust, at least, in their eyes. Alison and Shay took positions on either side of James close to the out-of-bounds line.

The bounty hunter grinned. His girls were instinctively ready to destroy his enemies, and it didn't bother him in the slightest.

Royce stepped back, raised his arm, and dropped it. "Kick ass, and take no prisoners. Show us who the true Mud Kings are."

The bounty hunters charged the Brownstone Family with a mighty roar. James rushed forward and slammed into the front line, grabbing two men and tossing them out past the line with ease before bowling several others over.

The desperate men tried to escape the long reach of their powerful boss, but he advanced on them with a hungry gleam in his eyes, plucking them from the mud and throwing them like they weighed nothing.

The men's attempt to dogpile James as a group ended with a good third of their team moaning or cursing outside the pit.

You guys should have been more careful.

Sensing the failure of the first strategy, several other men, one by one, tried to rush around James and tag his panels, their only hope at this point.

Shay spun as Lachlan and Max tried to tackle her. She grabbed the first man's arm and continued to turn with him before releasing her hold, and his redirected momentum sent him out of bounds. She ducked and slammed shoulder-first into Max, sending him out of the pit with a grunt.

"Damn," Max shouted as he hit the ground.

Alison waited, her hands behind her back as Shorty charged right at her.

"Nothing personal, but don't think I'm gonna show you mercy, little girl. There's no place for mercy in the pit."

She shrugged and waited until he was in front of her to leap to the side, splashing mud in her wake. The bounty hunter was two steps out of the pit before he realized what had even happened.

"Oh, man! You've got to be kidding me." Shorty kicked the ground.

A half-dozen other men charged James, hoping to go

for his panels, but in their greed, they ignored their flanks. Shay and Alison set upon them like hungry wolves, their quick hands moving from panel to panel. Four of the six let out cries of pain as they collapsed into the mud.

James grinned as he grabbed and flung the men still recovering from their shocks out of the pit. They landed with thuds and groans, some still twitching from the shocks.

Alison squeaked when a stray bounty hunter caught her by surprise. He didn't go for the panels, but instead picked the slender teen up and tossed her out of the pit.

She landed with a yelp and glared at the man, crossing her arms and frowning. "Avenge me!"

Shay took up the suggestion and shoved the gloating bounty hunter out of the ring when he was still focused on Alison. James cleaned up the rest.

The first round was over in less than eight minutes. The Brownstone Family had suffered one casualty, but the enemy had suffered over twenty.

Royce laughed. "Congratulations, men. You managed to take out one teen girl, and she actually took out or helped out several people before that. That's officially an ass-kicking."

The assembled bounty hunters mumbled under their breaths and shook their heads.

The drill instructor crossed his arms. "Spend a few minutes planning for the next round, so you don't embarrass yourselves again."

Trey stood up and wiped some mud off his face. "Staff Sergeant's right. We had no plan. Now let's go make a plan and show Mr. and Mrs. Brownstone and Kid Brownstone over there what we got goin' on."

James and Alison smirked.

Shay rolled her eyes. "Reminder… I'm just the girlfriend."

Ten minutes of harsh whispering later, both teams were back in the pit. James stood in the vanguard, Shay close behind and to his side. To the annoyance of Trey and his team, Alison stood way in the back. So much for their careful planning.

Trey leaned over to whisper to Shorty. "It's like they knew we were gonna flank."

Shorty shook his head. "It ain't no thing. We might not be able to take down Daddy Brownstone with a big rush, but we can take Little Brownstone, and then we can surround him and his woman."

He raised his hand, and Trey gave him a fist bump.

Trey raised a clenched fist into the air. "We're gonna show the Brownstone Family that we ain't no bitches."

Shay snickered.

The disorganized-looking line broke into three tight wedge formations. Trey charged at the front of the first wedge toward James, while the other two wedges rushed to either side of him. Small-group tactics, just like Royce had been trying to instill into them.

Alison laughed and thrust out with her hands. A purple wave of energy shot from her palms and smashed into the mud right in front of one of the flanking wedges. Mud splattered everywhere, blinding several of the men, who stumbled.

The magic itself distracted the other men, with the other side wedge collapsing in a mess as Isaiah slammed into leader Lachlan. Several men tumbled into the mud.

Trey kept his focus, but that was more than he could say for most of the men following him. When he got to James, he slid down and slapped a panel with a yell.

Just need Shorty and Max to...Wait, why the fuck am I the only one here?

Most of the men in his formation were standing several yards away.

You dumb motherfuckers. Pay attention to the target.

Trey ignored them and gritted his teeth.

James stared down at him, a smirk on his face. "Nice plan. Too bad it didn't work."

"Screw that. Smirk at this, big man." The junior bounty hunter nailed all three panels in rapid succession.

James grunted, and his face twitched, but he didn't go down.

Trey groaned. "Oh, hell no."

"Maybe if you did that a few times in a row, it might actually hurt."

"Come on, man."

His smile now gone, James reached down and yanked Trey up by his collar. The younger bounty hunter flailed in the other man's grip, but it didn't do any good. Trey had seen what James could do, and he knew his fate had already been sealed.

Trey let out a sigh, not even surprised once he was flying through the air toward a couple of the other guys standing at the side of the pit. He collided with them, and all three men tumbled out.

Cackling, Shay sprinted toward the collapsed side wedge on the opposite side as the men started standing up. She slapped panels with careful and precise movements. The screams and yells of men crying out in pain joined in an agonized symphony of defeat.

Another magical blast from Alison coated the men in the center with the mud. Three wiped it out of their eyes just in time for James to grab them and toss them like ragdolls out of bounds.

Trey scrubbed a hand over his face, dragging more mud down. "Shit. That was bad."

Royce marched over to the defeated team leader. "Got any thoughts?"

The bounty hunter stood and shook some mud off his hands. "It's the fucking Battle of Cannae, Staff Sergeant."

Royce laughed. "So you *do* pay attention when I talk." He shrugged. "I don't know about that, but right instincts. You don't lose a battle when you take a few hits. You lose a fight when you lose discipline, and no one sticks to the plan. That's when the casualties start piling up."

The First Battle of Camp Brownstone versus the Brownstone Family had taken eight minutes, with one casualty on the Brownstone Family side. The second was a massacre, lasting less than two, with zero casualties among the Brownstone Family.

Trey stood and shook his head. He surveyed his defeated men and laughed. They all eyed him like he'd lost his mind.

"Don't you get it? There ain't no shame in this. We work for the baddest-assed family in this whole country."

The shame drained from the men's face, and they grinned.

"Brownstone Family," they all chanted.

James, Alison, and Shay trudged out of the pit, grinning from ear to ear.

14

Tyler stepped into the Greek restaurant, glancing down at his silk vest and dress pants. His standard work outfit seemed fancy enough for brunch at an upscale Greek restaurant, but he was less concerned about what the restaurant staff thought and more about what Maria thought.

When did I start caring so much what a cop thinks about my clothes? Even if it is a hot, smart cop who doesn't take shit from anyone?

When he'd sent her a message about having found some information she suggested they meet, but rather than dinner, she wanted brunch. Something about being too busy at work to do dinner.

Was that a line? I haven't heard about any big high-level criminals in town. What the fuck is AET up to? Or is it just paperwork shit? Cops do *have to do a lot of paperwork.*

The hostess looked up from her podium with a smile. "Just you today, sir?"

Tyler shook his head and pointed inside. "My friend's already been seated. I can find my way there."

The woman looked over her shoulder toward the table where Maria sat in uniform. The cop waved.

"Very well, sir."

Tyler made his way over to Maria's table, enjoying the scents of anise, sumac, and coriander permeating the air, among other spices. He slid into a seat before taking a deep breath.

Maria nodded at a small tray of kalamata olive bread. "Thanks for meeting me, Tyler."

He took a bite of bread and swallowed. "So why no dinner? You got a bunch of work back at the station?"

"AET's on high alert, so I have to be at the station tonight." The cop shrugged.

"I've got my ear to the ground, and I haven't heard anything about anyone the AET should care about." He frowned, wondering how he could have missed something so obvious. "Why the high alert?"

Maria smirked. "You forgot the original threat. Surprised that you of all people would forget."

"Huh? What are you talking about?"

Maria leaned in and sighed. "LAPD's worried that if shit goes south at the hearing, Brownstone might...react poorly. They just want to have the maximum number of officers available in that case. I'll be at the hearing also. I have to testify anyway."

Tyler chuckled. "Really? That would be too funny for sure if Brownstone went nuts. It'd prove everything I've been saying, but it'd get pretty damned expensive, too."

She shrugged. "I don't get it. Half the LAPD's writing

the guy glowing recommendations, but the department still acts like he's going to kill everyone in that building if they look at him the wrong way."

"Is it really so weird? You believed that not all that long ago."

Maria took a sip of her water. "Things change, and people change." She set her glass down as the waitress approached.

After a quick discussion, their orders were in, and the waitress departed.

The cop returned her attention to Tyler. "So, tell me what you got for me, Mr. Big Information Broker."

"It took some digging, but the weird thing is this wasn't some random turnaround by the people who have been working Alison's case. Not that at all."

Maria frowned. "What do you mean?"

"The people who had been working her case were reassigned, and new people brought in at several levels, including the lawyers who might be involved, and the social workers who were monitoring her. It's like someone went in and cleaned house right before they started this whole anti-Brownstone crusade."

"That's suspicious. Damned suspicious."

Tyler nodded. "That's not the half of it. I found out the girl goes to a magic school out east, some government-sponsored one. It's not exactly secret, but it's not something they announce to the world, either. The fact she's even there kind of suggests some high-level people have her back, and from what I could find out, Brownstone's the one who pushed for her to go to the school."

"And you said it's government sponsored?" Maria

glanced around the room as if expecting CIA spies to be skulking at a table in trench coats. "Maybe that's the connection. Maybe someone wants Alison all to themselves and is trying to get Brownstone out of the way?"

Tyler shook his head. "I don't think so. She's been there since last fall. There were some minor road bumps in the adoption process earlier this summer, but this whole government-blocking-Brownstone thing is really recent, way after the school, way after the earlier stuff. It makes no sense to wait so long if that was the plan." Tyler took a deep breath then grinned. "And it gets better."

"Don't enjoy yourself too much."

"How can't I? Everyone says I'm the scumbag, but I love digging into the government and finding how they are the real criminals always getting away with the worst crimes."

Maria smirked. "No one loves a politician. Big surprise. What's your big reveal there?"

"There's a senator involved in this. I don't know which one, but it's pressure from that senator that got this anti-Brownstone ball rolling, and I'm talking from the federal senate, not the state." Tyler frowned. "And there was none of that pressure until this shit started, so it's not like they suddenly gave in. It's like not all that long ago this senator decided to fuck with Brownstone for some reason."

"What the hell? That's a lot of political muscle over one guy's adoption, even if it is Brownstone." Maria furrowed her brow and looked into her water glass. "Maybe this is part of some douchebag setting up a big win so he can run for president?"

Tyler shrugged a single shoulder. "Maybe, but why would he hide in the shadows then? Why not be loud and proud? There are other ways he could have screwed with Brownstone. Plus…"

"What?"

"You have cop instinct. I've got info broker instinct honed by years of experience." Tyler frowned.

Maria nodded slowly. "And what is that instinct telling you?"

"That there's something more here. Someone else. Someone's pushing the senator. I'd stake my bar on it." Tyler sat back and crossed his arms. "Just don't know who, and that's frustrating."

"Maybe some asshole criminal has blackmail material on the senator, someone Brownstone's tangled with before. A cartel guy, or left-over Harriken. Someone like that." Maria shrugged. "Guess it doesn't matter for now. Just knowing this is coming from a senator helps. I'll talk to people at my end. Maybe we can figure something out. This has been helpful. Someone's getting very lucky tonight."

Tyler blinked several times at the grinning woman, both excited and too scared at the same time to ask if she meant him.

Helping Brownstone's earning me fringe benefits I never thought I'd get.

He grinned back.

***

The man tapped his boxing gloves against Alison's and glanced at Shay. "You sure about this? I can hold back."

Shay nodded. "Don't hold back much. It's pointless if you do."

Alison sighed and raised her gloves.

Her energy sight wasn't enough to give her careful tracking of someone in a hand-to-hand fight, but she wouldn't be nailed without seeing it coming. A kickboxing sparring match was a nice training exercise.

The tomb raider grinned to herself, but winning, at least in the first bout, wasn't even the point. Alison had already come a long way, and Shay needed to push her a bit farther down the path of true independence.

The teen moved forward, throwing a few jabs at the man. He blocked with little effort, letting his opponent keep up her attacks, a growing smirk on his face. He responded with a few weak kicks, but she jumped back each time, dodging them.

The teen managed to get in a body blow, and bounced back with a grin. "This isn't so hard."

Shay sighed.

He's toying with you, kid. Don't get cocky now. You're nowhere good enough to get cocky yet.

Alison's opponent repaid her comment with a powerful side hook. The force of the blow had her spinning, and she collapsed to the ground with a yelp.

The man slammed his gloves together. "Kickboxing's no game, little girl. If you're going to get into the ring, you better take it seriously."

Shay sighed. "Get up."

Alison pushed off the ground. "Dad's going to freak if I come home with a black eye, you know."

The tomb raider patted her pocket. She hadn't shown it

to Alison, but she'd brought a healing potion. "Don't worry, I've got a little something for that. Once I'm done, there'll be nothing bad left."

It was an expensive way to finish up her sparring, but the girl was right. James wanted her training and learning to be independent, but if Shay brought her home with her eye swollen shut and her lip split, he'd probably march right over to the Steel Gloves gym, and level the place with his bare hands. That was after he got done leveling every warehouse Shay owned in an angry rage.

He was like a lot of dads. He wanted his girl to be strong and independent, but he also wanted to lock her up in a tower and protect her from anyone who might even make her feel bad.

Alison sighed. "I don't even understand what this is supposed to be teaching me. There's a reason boxers fight people who are the same size."

"What it's teaching you, little girl, is how to take a punch and get back up."

"This is just unfair."

Shay snorted. "Unfair? Fights are often unfair. Thugs and muggers don't pick targets who look like they can beat them. Learning to protect yourself is about learning to accept that nothing is ever fair, so you need to do what you can to even the odds."

The teen rubbed her swelling cheek with her glove. "Wow, tough love, Aunt Shay."

Shay leaned over until she was right at Alison's ear and could whisper, "Okay, you did it my way with no magic, but in the real world, if you're in a fight, you use whatever tool you have to win. Like I said, even the odds. So, round two, you do what you need to do."

Alison nodded and headed into the ring. "Where you going?"

Her opponent was already half-way over the rope. "What? Seriously?"

The teen gave him her best angry glare and shook her head. "I'm more serious than I've ever been. We're not done."

He laughed. "You didn't get enough the first time? I was holding back, and you still went down like nothing."

"You afraid? If you're afraid, that's okay. Feel free to run away."

His smile vanished. "I told you kickboxing isn't no game, kid." He sneered and looked at Shay. "I thought you said she was some sort of magic chick, but this is embarrassing. Don't blame me if she ends up getting hurt."

Shay feigned yawning. "You want her to use magic? You sure?"

"Better than beating down some toothpick and calling it a victory."

The tomb raider shrugged. "Let's keep the screaming down to a minimum, then."

He snorted. "That's on her. I'm not holding back anymore."

"Oh, you don't get it. I wasn't talking to *you*. I was talking to her." The tomb raider grinned.

The man immediately rushed toward Alison. She yanked off her left glove and held up her hand. The man brought his arm back to throw a punch, but a bright flash from her hand blinded him. He stumbled back with a grunt and shielded his eyes.

The girl didn't give him a chance to recover. She rushed forward and delivered a series of quick blows to his face and body. She spun into a roundhouse kick, just like Shay had shown her at her warehouse during their last training session.

The man's initial quick forward motion served him poorly. He stepped right into the girl's foot, providing just enough extra force for his head to snap back. He groaned and slumped to his knees before falling forward with a thump.

Alison tilted her head. "As Sun Tzu said, 'Appear weak when you are strong, and strong when you are weak.'"

Shay climbed through the ropes and over to Alison, snickering. She patted the girl on the shoulder. "Oh, they got that Marine filling you with all that ancient wisdom crap, too?"

"Why? What would *you* say about this situation?"

The tomb raider grinned. "Sometimes it's better to be lucky than good." She glanced at a clock on the wall. "We better get you back home and cleaned up. The last thing James needs is to be late for the hearing."

The man on the ground pushed up slowly, still groaning.

Shay offered him a wave. "Better luck next time."

Shay stepped out of her Fiat and made her way toward the courthouse. James and Alison had already exited his truck in a parking spot closer to the front, and they were heading to the stairs leading to the courthouse.

Although Shay liked the look of James in his black suit, the discomfort on his face and the way he kept tugging at his jacket made his opinion of the clothes clear.

She swallowed and wondered if it was smart for her to be entering a place with cameras like this, but given her experiences with the CIA, it was obvious that Peyton's efforts had done enough to create a fake background that wasn't so easily pierced. If anyone dug into her background, they'd just find that she was a professor at UCLA who specialized in archaeology and revised history.

She took a few deep breaths as she reminded herself of that.

Shay stopped and let out a long sigh when she spotted a half-dozen drones circling the area.

Of course, the damned media vultures would be out for this. The State of California versus the Scourge of Harriken. How could they not show up?

It didn't matter. She didn't give a shit about them getting their scoop.

She pulled out her phone and dialed Peyton.

"What's up?" the hacker answered.

"A swarm of news drones, from the looks of it, at the courthouse." Shay frowned. "I want them all down."

"All of them? You sure?"

"Yeah."

Peyton laughed. "Someone doesn't like being on the news."

"This is more for James' sake. I don't want these fuckers lucking into him doing something stupid and splashing it all over the world. One wrong move and the government can take the girl from him, but that's gonna involve him destroying half of Los Angeles. This is not just for his sake, but for the city's."

"Okay, fair enough." The click of typing came over the line. "Just give me a few minutes."

Shay made her way slowly toward the stairs, a smirk on her face as she awaited the doom of the drones. These news assholes got high ratings, clicks, and readership from writing about James, but the minute they had a chance, they turned on him and started writing rude stories about Alison.

You get what you deserve, vultures. I hope those things are insured.

Peyton chuckled. "I'm too good."

Shay glanced up. "I don't see anything hap—"

The drones' rotors all cut out at once, and they spiraled to the ground.

The tomb raider snickered, imagining a bunch of panicked drone operators sitting in their control rooms watching tens of thousands of dollars fall to the ground. The machines smashed when they hit, pieces flying everywhere.

Yeah, that's got to hurt.

Shay snickered. "And one last thing…"

15

J ames and Alison waited outside the courthouse until Shay caught up. She sauntered up the stairs with a huge grin on her face, whistling a peppy tune.

Yeah. I thought so.

"You look too damned happy." James looked past her to make sure she hadn't kicked the shit out of some random mugger on the way there. "Or are you the reason all those drones just fell?"

"Strange things happen when you rely on technology too much." She shrugged. "Anyway, we won't have a problem with drones or external news footage for the next few hours. I'm guessing a lot of cameras are also going to have some trouble uploading their footage today. Just saying…"

Alison rolled her eyes. "Overkill much, Aunt Shay?"

"Always prepare the battlefield ahead of time." Shay winked. "I'm sure Sun Tzu said something like that."

James nodded toward the dense pack of reporters standing inside. "I think they only haven't come after us because they want to wait until we get inside. Enter the belly of the beast."

"Might as well give them what they want, then. We just need to walk past them. It's not like they can block you from going to the courtroom."

"Oriceran freak!" someone screamed from above.

James' head snapped up. A grinning man was leaning out the third-story window, flipping them off. "Yeah, I heard about it. Fucking freak little girl that Brownstone wants to adopt. Not even human. Fuck you. Go back to Oriceran." The man ducked inside the window and ran toward the other end of the building.

Alison sighed and looked down.

The bounty hunter gritted his teeth. Fucking with him was one thing, but screwing with his daughter was another. Screw self-control.

I'm gonna fuck tear you apart, asshole.

"Don't do anything, James." Shay placed a hand on his shoulder. "I wouldn't be surprised if he's been paid to try and make you overreact. I'll take care of him. Peyton's got the drones and cameras in this area disabled."

"Meaning what?" James growled.

"Meaning I can go wherever I need to without looking suspicious. I'll make sure this guy regrets screwing with Alison."

The girl looked up with a pained smile.

James gave Shay a nod. He'd do anything to protect Alison, but he also knew that Shay was better about delivering pain in a way that didn't end with her getting caught.

He grunted and opened the door, motioning Alison through before entering himself. He nodded to Shay, and she gave him a little salute before jogging off to the side of the building and glancing up at another open third-story window near the end of the building.

Huh. Time for Parkour Penny?

Like a dense school of fish, the dozens of reporters inside the courthouse turned as one, shoving out microphones while their camera operators flipped on their equipment. Everyone was eager for that dramatic clip they could run for the next few days.

Given what Shay said, I wonder if they can record but not transmit, or if Peyton's hacking their computers somewhere else. Huh. Don't know. Maybe it's best that way.

Sorry, assholes. I'm not gonna flip out and give you what you want.

"Mr. Brownstone, Mr. Brownstone," shouted a reporter.

James put his arm over Alison's shoulder as he marched through the thicket, ignoring all the questions and keeping his expression neutral. He'd leave it to Shay to handle the heckling asshole.

***

Shay finishing jogging around the side of the building. Fortunately, there wasn't anyone on the small side street, but she doubted that would last for long. She needed to move fast.

After a final quick check for witnesses, she broke into a sprint. She jumped and grabbed an air conditioning window unit, swinging back and forth before jumping to another unit.

She pulled herself up and leapt off the unit toward a

small ledge on the second floor. She swung back and forth a few times to build up momentum and swung up to another ledge on the corner of the building.

This is almost too easy.

The tomb raider climbed around the edge of the building and grabbed the edge of the open window. It was some sort of storage room filled with cardboard boxes on shelves. She waited a few seconds and then jumped from the ledge into the building, rolling a few feet before hopping to her feet.

I guess I could always start a second career as a cat burglar like Marcus if I ever felt like it.

Shay threw open the door and sprinted in the direction she'd last seen the heckler. A few seconds later she spotted the man running down a hallway. She looked back and forth and grinned. No witnesses.

That made everything even easier than she'd hoped. Now she wouldn't have to fake anything to justify beating him down.

Shay continued charging, and the man blinked, surprised to see her suddenly on the third floor.

"Hey, asshole, remember me?" she shouted.

The man skidded to a start and sneered. "You got up here quick. What? Oriceran magic shit? Probably. Fucking traitor bitch."

Shay sauntered up to the man, grinning the entire time, though it didn't reach her eyes. "When you're as good as I am, you don't need magic." She sighed. "But here's the problem. You insulted that girl, and I care a lot about that, so I can't let it go. Her dad there wants to punt you through a wall. I'm not gonna do that, but you are gonna feel a little pain."

"Screw you, bitch. Earth is for humans. The Oricerans shouldn't even be here. Fuck off, we're full."

The tomb raider let out a long sigh and then looked around. Perfect position. No cameras in the hall. It was like the universe wanted her to beat the man down.

Shay gave the man a cool smile. "Last chance. Apologize."

"I'm not going to apologize for defending the Earth from Oriceran freaks. I'm a proud Earthling."

"An Earthling? Geeze, that sounds fucking lame." Shay took a step forward. "And Alison was born here, asshole."

"Doesn't change the fact that she's a—"

Shay threw a fist into his stomach, and the man's eyes bulged as he doubled over. She slammed her knee into his nose, enjoying the crunch before she dropped his unconscious ass to the floor.

The tomb raider took a few deep breaths, resisting the urge to break a few more bones. It'd be satisfying, but she didn't need police attention, even with her currently CIA-proof background.

If we were in an alley at night, I probably would have crippled you, asshole. You're damned fucking lucky.

She knelt and ran her hands through his pockets. She found a butterfly knife, not the kind of thing he was allowed to have in a courthouse. She left the weapon in plain sight and jogged away.

Eventually, someone would find him, and even if he tried to complain about her beating him up, he'd still have to explain his illegal weapon. Now he'd have to deal with a broken nose and jail.

Next time just apologize, asshole.

James' lawyer straightened a pile of papers on the table in the conference room and placed them back into his briefcase, a grim look on his face.

Shay, James, and Alison sat opposite the man at a long table. The hearing was going to start in less than fifteen minutes.

James balled his hands into fists.

This is the beginning of everything. We can do this. We can win. Fuck the government. I won't let them take Alison from me.

The lawyer's expression softened. "The statements of support I've received from the community have been very, very helpful, and I'm confident that these witnesses will have nothing but good things to say about you. The state's complaints rest mostly on concerns about your profession, but the fact that you have so many law enforcement officers speaking on your behalf does a lot to blunt that line of attack. It's just hard for them to claim you're some sort of clear and present danger when the local police and even local priests claim the opposite."

The bounty hunter grunted. "Sounds good, then. Right?"

"The state's documentation doesn't support the idea that they had a problem, so that also undermines their case. That is, they had no issue with the girl staying with you before, so it's a bit rich for them to suddenly complain.

They had plenty of opportunities to take her." The lawyer shook his head. "Most of their evidence involves video clips of you fighting bounties or committing property destruction. There are only a few people they're going to put on the stand who are worrying me."

"Like who?"

The lawyer frowned. "For one, the AET lieutenant, Maria Hall. Her official reports aren't always kind to you."

James grunted. "Yeah, I thought she didn't have it in for me anymore, but I guess I blew that by upsetting her recently."

Fuck. Is she pissed over the whole Tyler thing? Maybe I fucked up more than I realized. Damn it.

"Don't worry. We have a pile of statements from other officers, and several of them will be testifying." The lawyer held up his finger. "The point is, Mr. Brownstone, as long as you don't make a scene, we should be good. That's also why we're going to avoid having you testify unless absolutely necessary. It'd be far too easy for the government lawyer to trip you up and make you look like a maniac on the stand. They'll be calling several of your associates to ask questions, but I'll be able to respond to those attacks."

James frowned. "Why does everyone keep assuming I'm gonna make a scene?"

Shay sighed and looked at Alison. "Explain it to him, kid."

The girl placed her hand over his. "Dad, you're James Brownstone. You're the Scourge of Harriken, the Granite Ghost. A class-six bounty hunter. Your way of saying 'hi' is kicking someone through a door."

"That's not true, unless someone…" He shrugged.

"Okay, so it often is. Big deal. I don't deal with nice people. I deal with people like the Red-Eyes Killer or King Pyro. You can't talk them down. I've been trying to be more polite because tactically it's smart, but it just doesn't work so well, so I still have to kick ass a lot of the time."

The lawyer cleared his throat loudly. "Be that as it may, Mr. Brownstone. This won't be a situation where kicking ass, as you put it, will be necessary. Understood?"

James grunted. "Yeah. Let's just get this shit over with."

When James, Alison, and Shay stepped inside, the bounty hunter blinked at the number of people crammed into the small family courtroom. It was filled to capacity, but at least there were no news cameras.

He didn't recognize several people, but the look in their eyes made him think they were either criminals or bounty hunters. Among the more recognizable people present, in addition to hungry-looking reporters, was Sergeant Mack, along with several other cops, including Detectives West and Lafayette from Las Vegas. Charlyce, Trey, Shorty, Royce, and a few other of his guys were there. Father McCartney gave him a polite nod from the corner.

Good to have people who actually believe in me here.

Lieutenant Hall sat beside Tyler near the front, a frown on her face. James didn't know if that was a good thing, given that the state's lawyer was calling her up to testify. She'd hated his guts for so long, it was hard for him to trust that she wouldn't take this chance to screw with him.

And hell, the mere presence of the information broker made his stomach tighten.

Why the fuck would Tyler come to my hearing? Since when does he care about this shit? Or did he give the government evidence against me? Maybe he thinks that if he can fuck up my adoption, it'll be revenge or some shit like that. If I find out he helped them, I'm gonna tear that bar apart.

A large contingent of Oricerans were interspersed in the crowd, mostly dwarves, Light Elves, and Wood Elves, which made sense, given that they represented some of the larger local communities. James didn't recognize most of them, but he did recognize the Los Angeles consul, Yev.

Fuck Tyler. Why is that consulate guy here? Does this have something to do with Alison being half-Oriceran? The lawyer didn't say shit about the Oricerans caring much, except the ones who wanted to help me. Is he here to help?

James frowned and took a seat at a front table with Alison and his lawyer. Shay wasn't testifying or a party to the hearing, so she took a seat in the gallery right behind James. Cold looks from Shay and James had a reporter giving up his seat and scurrying out of the room.

The judge, a stern-looking older black man with salt-and-pepper hair, banged his gavel to call the hearing into session. "We're here today to discuss the adoption of one Alison Anderson by James Brownstone. Let me be clear what this hearing is, and is not. This is solely to determine the suitability of James Brownstone as a guardian for this girl as part of his adoption request. This isn't a criminal trial, and Mr. Brownstone is not a defendant. I'm aware of the high-profile nature of this case, but that doesn't matter.

This is a courtroom, and the laws of the State of California will be duly applied."

A murmur swept through the crowd but died under the withering look of the judge.

The state's lawyer, Davis, stood up and adjusted his tie, a vulpine smile on his face. "I'd like to start with our first ten exhibits, Your Honor."

Fucking asshole. Why do you look so happy? At least have the decency to look like they forced you to do it.

The smug Davis smiled and stopped the current video. He pointed toward the frozen explosion on the large LCD screen hanging in the corner of the room. A few Harriken leaping away from the explosion were clear in the video, along with glass, metal, and wood debris from the impact of James' opening assault on the Harriken building.

"Your Honor, as you can see, I want this record to reflect that Mr. Brownstone used a military-grade weapon to blow the building open during his raid on the Harriken."

"Duly noted." The judge looked at James' lawyer. "And your comments on this, Mr. Silverberg?"

James' lawyer cleared his throat. "To remind the court, and as I noted in the statements we previously submitted to the court, Mr. Brownstone acknowledges using those weapons during that encounter. He's a class-six bounty hunter, and has the appropriate licenses for all types of weapons that have been documented in all these exhibits." He nodded toward the screen. "And I'd like to draw the court's attention to the fact that a dozen police officers are also visible in the frame, and many more were present on site. This wasn't some surreptitious nighttime assault, but a sanctioned organizational dead-or-alive bounty conducted with the full knowledge and cooperation of the LAPD."

The judge scribbled down a few notes. "Duly noted."

Davis rolled his eyes and looked away.

Keep being smug, asshole. It's just my life and my kid's you're trying to ruin.

A few minutes of back and forth discussion passed before a new clip was played. In the latest clip, King Pyro crashed through a bank window, and James followed. Their vicious brawl continued until James finished him off by smashing the man's head into the asphalt and permanently ending the man's threat.

Several people in the gallery winced and gasped at the violence on display.

James didn't flinch. He didn't care about killing King Pyro. That guy was a murdering asshole, and he'd threatened his family. He'd gotten what was coming to him.

This is what it means to go after high-level bounties. Can't win by beating them at a game of cards.

Davis sighed. "To me, this looks like premeditated murder or at least a lack of restraint. From the looks of it, Mr. Brownstone had already won, but continued assaulting him up to the point he died."

A murmur broke out among several of the cops and bounty hunters sitting in the viewing gallery.

The judge looked at James' lawyer and nodded.

Silverberg shook his head. "Again, I wish to point out the many fine men and women in blue in the video. This dangerous felon, Jordan Adams AKA King Pyro, was not just a bank robber, but a murderer who killed without restraint, including children. I also feel compelled to point out that given dozens of police officers were watching this battle unfold, including a fully-equipped AET team. If they felt Mr. Brownstone had crossed the line, they had ample opportunity to arrest him.

James grunted. The AET had been close to doing just that. He glanced at Lieutenant Hall. Would she say something like that when she testified?

Fuck King Pyro. That motherfucker got what he had coming to him, and they expect me to feel bad that I did that? How many girls like Alison did I save by taking the asshole out?

No, James refused to feel bad for taking out the trash. The only other option was to let it sit, fester, and stink up the entire city.

16

The dramatic footage kept coming: highway drone footage of James having a shootout with hitmen, multiple videos of James throwing people through windows or punching, kicking, or shooting them, not to mention so many explosions that Michael Bay should have come out of retirement and sued James for stealing his directing style.

James scrubbed a hand over his face. When the government played them all close together, it made him look like he was the most dangerous man on the planet.

Maybe I fucking am, but it doesn't matter.

For years, he'd prided himself on this reputation and the power of terror he could wield against criminals and bounties. He'd never anticipated that the same reputation could be turned against him and used to steal his daughter from him.

Fuck them. Fuck all of them.

At least his lawyer did a good job of explaining away each clip. The argument was always the same. The police were in full support of James, and given the dangerous nature of the criminals involved, it was unlikely they could have been taken down any other way. It also happened to be true.

The bounty hunter's stomach was twisting in on itself when the last video ended, and the government lawyer called Lieutenant Hall to the stand.

James gritted his teeth. Here it came.

Oh, shit. She's gonna rant about that pay-per-view thing and make me look like an irresponsible idiot. Nothing I did ever put that girl at risk, you assholes.

The clerk finished swearing Lieutenant Hall in, and the government lawyer sauntered over to her.

Davis shot a grin at James.

If you're trying to get me to pound your face in, keep it up, asshole. Maybe Shay can handle you later.

The lawyer smiled. "Lieutenant Hall, you're the primary tactical leader of the Los Angeles Police Department's Anti-Enhanced Threat team, correct?"

She nodded. "That is correct. I have been for several years."

"And you and your team have handled a variety of threats, including dangerous magical threats like the perpetrator of the Farmer's Market Massacre, Tessa Vansant."

"That is also correct."

James gripped the table so hard the wood started to crack.

The government lawyer adjusted his tie. James didn't even get what all the showboating was for. The judge had allowed some media inside, but there were no cameras allowed. Maybe he just wanted the reporters to write up how suave he was or something like that.

"So, as a police officer and an expert in dealing with dangerous high-level threats, often of a magical nature," the lawyer began, "can you give us your opinion on how James Brownstone has handled these incidents as shown in the videos we've submitted into evidence?"

The lieutenant leaned forward and smiled. "I'd be happy to."

James glanced at Alison. She didn't look frightened. Instead, she was shooting an angry glare at the government lawyer. There was a good chance that it wouldn't be Daddy Brownstone who lost control if things continued the way they were going.

Don't worry, kid. I'm not leaving you, no matter what.

The cop coughed and cleared her throat. "First of all, I want to congratulate Mr. Brownstone on his restraint. I personally understand how difficult it can be to show restraint in these types of situations."

Davis blinked. "W-what? I want to remind you, Lieutenant Hall, that I've reviewed your various case reports and some of your personal notes in regards to these incidents. Many of your reports criticize the level of force used by Mr. Brownstone, along with the level of property damage he inflicted."

Lieutenant Hall smiled. "The thing about taking a bunch of incidents and reducing them to a few minutes and a freeze frame here and there is that it removes all the context of the fundamental dangers of the unfolding situation. Quite frankly, that's dangerous and ignorant." She sighed and shrugged. "The reality is that during a dangerous tactical situation involving magical forces, you can't always wait to come up with the right and easy answer. Every person and being who uses magic is unique and represents a challenge to even highly-trained personnel. The only thing that a good bounty hunter or cop should be concerned about is how to minimize the collateral damage to people. Lives are always more important than property."

The man's face reddened, and he looked at the judge. "Your Honor, I think that perhaps Lieutenant Hall should be dismissed. Some of her statements are inconsistent with her previous reports, and she should be held in contempt of court for perjury."

The cops in the gallery all grumbled under their breath, and Tyler glared at the government lawyer.

The judge shook his head. "I've reviewed her statements, and I'll take everything into account when making my final ruling, but nothing she's saying here is proof of perjury, which I should remind counsel is a serious charge."

Lieutenant Hall snorted. "Things only seem different because I was examining them in isolation and didn't see the larger pattern. I don't deny anything I reported earlier, but I'm now offering a big-picture overview of how I see Mr. Brownstone's behavior and conduct as a bounty hunter."

Davis marched over to her and tried to loom over her.

James almost laughed. The woman strapped on armor and faced magical killers and monsters, and some stuffed shirt in a suit thought he could intimidate her? Hell, for that matter, Hall had gotten in *James'* face, and he was a lot tougher than any government lawyer.

"Lieutenant," the lawyer hissed, "need I remind you of the danger that James Brownstone represents to the community? You've personally commented on it several times."

The AET officer crossed her arms and stared the lawyer down. "Danger? You know what a danger is? A danger is some crazy-ass witch who marches into a farmer's market, summons demons, and starts killing people. A danger is a pyromancer who thinks nothing of murdering families." She shot up, her eyes blazing with anger. "Look through every report I've ever written and show me anywhere where I've ever claimed Brownstone killed someone other than a criminal. You won't find a single instance."

The judge leveled a stern gaze at Hall. "Sit down, Lieutenant."

The cop took a deep breath and sat. "I'm sorry, Your Honor."

Davis shook a finger. "Lieutenant, that's not the point. The man is a menace and a threat to the public order." The lawyer pointed at Alison. "And there's no way he should be entrusted with the care of a teenage girl with a difficult past."

Alison rolled her eyes.

Lieutenant Hall barked a laugh. "A threat to public order? A menace? These high-powered assholes don't care about anything but spreading death. That Tessa Vansant? She was a nutjob who killed people because she was half-convinced they weren't really alive. King Pyro didn't give a crap who got in the way. The Harriken were ruthless criminals involved in everything from drugs to human trafficking." She cut through the air with her hand. "Don't you get it? This isn't the world we grew up in. The return of magic has changed everything, and people need to get that through their thick skulls."

The lawyer gritted his teeth. "I don't think that's re—"

"Relevant?" The lieutenant shook her head. "It used to be the worst thing a cop might run into was a terrorist or some nutjob who built himself a tank. Now we have people who can fly, teleport, and make fireballs appear with wands or just their hands. We have necromancers who can bring the dead back to life." She pointed at the lawyer, trembling with anger. "Until twenty years ago, we lived in a world where a normal person with a gun was at the top of the food chain. That world's gone, and now we're back to being in the jungle, naked and afraid. You know what I'm going to do if I'm in the jungle naked and afraid? I'm going to go find myself a jaguar and befriend it, and I'll hide behind that jaguar while it stops all the other hungry animals that want to chomp down on me and the people around me."

Davis blinked. "A jaguar? This is ridiculous."

The cop shook her head. "The world isn't safe, and it won't be for a long time. If LA's a little safer, if we can sleep a little bit easier at night without thinking some crazy demon-summoning witch will murder us when we buy honey at a farmers' market, it's because of James Brownstone, and blocking his adoption of that girl would disgust me as a cop, a woman, an American. The government should be ashamed for doing this to him, and should be apologizing to him for putting him through this."

Father McCartney started clapping. Sergeant Mack joined him, along with Charlyce and the Camp Brownstone bounty hunters. Soon, almost everyone was clapping, even one guy in the corner who James was pretty sure was a member of the 25K Triad. The lack of clapping among several of the Oricerans, including Consul Yev, was noticeable.

The judge banged his gavel several times. "Order in the court. Order in the court."

The clapping died down, and the lawyer stared at Lieutenant Hall, slack-jawed.

The judge looked between the two. "Do you have anything else you wanted to ask, counselor?"

The lawyer shook his head and threw up a hand in disgust. "I've no further use for this witness."

James blinked several times, unsure what the hell had just happened. Everyone told him that he shouldn't make a scene, but damned if the AET lieutenant hadn't done just that.

The judge banged his gavel. "We'll take a fifteen minutes recess so everyone can calm down."

Several people rose and started to file out.

James looked at his lawyer. "Was that good or bad? I can't tell."

Silverberg chuckled. "A woman who has reams of notes saying that you're a dangerous man risked contempt of court to declare as a cop, a woman, and American that you're a good man. Yeah, that's good. It's very damned good."

Alison reached over to pat James' hand. "It'll be okay, Dad. That government lawyer's not a nice man. I can see all the greed and ambition in his soul."

The lawyer looked at James, and he just shook his head in response. They didn't need to go into this at court.

"We just have to keep presenting the other side," the lawyer offered. "And everything will be fine."

A few minutes passed with light chatter between Alison, Shay, and James before everyone returned and the judge restarted the hearing.

The government lawyer had his smug smile back on. He called Sergeant Mack to the stand, and soon the man was sworn in.

Trey flexed his hands. He'd been clenching his fist and resisting the urge to march over to the smug prick trying to make James look bad and lay him out.

Fucker. How dare you do the big man like that?

The lawyer folded his hands behind his back as he glanced back at Trey, Shorty, and the others.

What now, bitch? You've got some character assassination you need to do on us? Bring it, asshole.

He pointed to Trey. "Do you recognize that man, Sergeant Mack?"

Sergeant Mack nodded. "Yes. That's Trey Garfield."

"And you recognize the men sitting near him?"

"Yes. I do. They are associates of his, and have been for some time."

The lawyer nodded slowly. "And isn't it true that these men are all members of a street gang?"

Sergeant Mack shook his head. "No, sir. That is not correct."

The lawyer's head snapped toward the cop. "Excuse me? May I remind you that you're under oath, Sergeant."

"With the Lord as my witness, I'm not lying." The cop took a deep breath. "They *used* to be members of a street gang, but they no longer are. In fact, I know for a fact from an associate of mine, Detective Delroy Washington of the anti-gang taskforce, that Trey Garfield and all his active associates have been removed from the official list of known gang members in Los Angeles County. So, as far as the LAPD is concerned, they aren't gang members."

Davis took a deep breath, a vein bulging in his head. "Be that as it may, they were in fact, until recently, members of a known street gang. So, it wouldn't be incorrect to say that James Brownstone associates with criminals."

Sergeant Mack shook his head "That's inaccurate. Those men are no longer criminals. They work as licensed bounty hunters. They hunt down criminals. They are not criminals themselves."

"I've got statements here discussing how when James Brownstone's home was being rebuilt, these criminals were acting as local toughs and threatening people, and at least some locals suggest they were stealing building supplies."

The lawyer continued, listing a myriad of the sins, real and imagined, of Trey's gang.

Trey started to rise, but Aunt Charlyce shoved him down with her hand.

"What the hell you thinking you doing, boy?" she whispered.

"That motherfucker's twisting everything around," Trey whispered back. "I've got something to say, and a nice, shiny shoe to shove up his ass."

Aunt Charlyce rolled her eyes. "He's a lawyer. That's what they do. The Devil himself is probably afraid to talk to lawyers. Probably sends them straight to heaven just to be safe, and a court of law is no place to put your shoe up anyone's ass to make a point."

Trey glanced at James. The big man's face was red, and he looked like he wanted to pick up the table in front of him and crack it over the lawyer's head.

I feel you, James. I feel you.

Sergeant Mack laughed, cutting into the government lawyer's parade of horrible anecdotes. "You know at one point, those criminals as you're calling them, phoned the police to help us stop some dangerous gang members in that neighborhood. So, you're telling me that James Brownstone associates with criminals, but what I see is a bunch of young men who now have legitimate jobs and respect the police enough to work with them to stop crime before it happens." He shook his head. "Most so-called normal citizens don't even do that. They don't want to be involved, and—"

"That will be enough," Davis snapped. "I'm through with this witness."

The cop gave the judge a polite nod.

The judge looked at James' lawyer. "Counselor, do you have any questions for Sergeant Mack?"

"Not at this time, your honor."

The judge nodded. "The witness is dismissed."

Sergeant Mack stood and made his way back to the gallery

Davis grinned at Trey. "I call Trey Garfield to the stand."

Trey snorted and marched to the witness stand, adjusting his tie to make sure it was perfect before sitting. He was sworn in and glared defiantly at the lawyer.

You made a mistake, you stupid motherfucker. Get ready to face the smoothest fucking Trey who's ever lived.

The lawyer sighed. "We already established that you were in a gang, so I won't bother going over that again. I want to ask you instead about why you work for Mr. Brownstone?"

The bounty hunter gave the lawyer a thin smile. "Taking down scumbags and criminals gives me a feeling of accomplishment."

"It's not because it lets you be a violent thug and get away with it?"

Trey took a deep breath and slowly let it out. "No, that's not accurate, sir. I'd go so far as to say it's completely *inaccurate.*"

I'll show you violent thug, you smug son of a bitch.

Davis clucked his tongue. "It's just a bit much to believe, you know? That some hardened gang leader turns over a new leaf and decides to become a good guy just because a bounty hunter asks him to?"

Trey chuckled quietly. "Ever read any Marcus Aurelius?"

"Marcus Aurelius?"

"Yes. Oh, I'm sorry, I assumed a man of your education would know about him. Roman emperor, famous follower of the Stoic philosophy. Apparently, they didn't cover that in law school when they were teaching you how to sue fast-food places."

Scattered laughs erupted from the gallery.

The lawyer's face reddened. "I know who Marcus Aurelius is, Mr. Garfield. My question is, how is he relevant to the matter of James Brownstone and your criminal past?"

Trey grinned. "Well, as *that man* said, 'The universe is change. Our life is what our thoughts make it.' Who am I to question the wisdom of a Stoic Roman emperor?"

More laughter followed.

The bounty hunter nodded at James. "I don't deny that I was a criminal, but Mr. Brownstone showed me a better path. He didn't have to. He could've treated me like a piece of garbage, but instead, he showed me respect and held out a hand when I needed it, so I left the street and became better."

"I don't care about that, Mr. Garfield—"

"He gave me a hand up instead of a handout," Trey continued, raising his voice. "And allowed me to shift from being street trash to the kind of man who can sit in court and quote Marcus Aurelius."

It took all Trey's self-control not to add "fucking" between the Marcus and Aurelius.

The government lawyer just stared at Trey, his eyes narrowed and hatred on his face.

Trey leaned in and grinned. "If you want me to say that James Brownstone associates with criminals, then, yeah, I'll say it loud and proud. James Brownstone associates with criminals, and many of those criminals, after dealing with him, realize that being a criminal is the path to ending up dead or in prison. Everyone in my gang is now not only law-abiding but taking down other criminals. That means that just by him being around, not even doing his normal thing, he's making this city and country safer. Now, any other questions, counselor?"

Take that, motherfucker.

17

Trey's testimony was finished, and the lawyer called up Charlyce.

A few minutes into the woman's testimony, Davis was again red-faced and looked like he wanted to slap another Garfield.

Charlyce gave him a soft smile. "Yes, I admit that I was homeless, and addicted to drugs. I admit to everything you just talked about. I was a shame to my family, myself, and the Lord, but you know what, Mr. Davis? I found God again, and then I found James Brownstone. And now, not only do I not live on the street, I have a full-time job, and I volunteer every week at an orphanage. Mr. Brownstone helped me, just like he helped my nephew. A hand up, not a hand out."

Davis frowned. "How do we know you're not still involved in drugs?"

"I will gladly submit to any drug testing the court or police want. My only drug is Jesus now." She nodded and gave the lawyer a happy smile. "You could use a little church, I think, Mr. Davis."

The gallery laughed, and the lawyer gritted his teeth.

"I'm done with this witness."

The judge looked at Silverberg, who had a big grin on his face.

"I think Miss Garfield has already made everything abundantly clear."

Davis watched, disdain in his eyes, as Charlyce made her way off the stand. "Your Honor, I'd now ask that the court clerk read my next submitted exhibit, and I need the computer queued up to the next set of video clips."

James scrubbed a hand down his face. Things had been going well enough, between Trey and Charlyce's testimony, but now things had shifted the other way as the court clerk read a police after-action report concerning the bounty hunter's fight with Lars Hansen in the desert, punctuated with clips from the fight in all its brutal glory.

Fucking cops seizing all that footage. Guess I should have figured that shit would come back to bite me in the ass. I never thought it would be this way.

The clerk finished reading the report, and Davis shrugged.

"Your honor, I think the police report and video clips speak for themselves. Mr. Brownstone basically challenged this Lars Hansen to a duel to lure him out to the desert and then murdered him. We see a pattern here of a merciless killer who takes lives when he has other options. A dangerous man, who shouldn't be anywhere around a young girl."

Alison kept her lips pursed and continued giving the government lawyer a death glare.

The judge nodded and scribbled a few notes. He looked at Silverberg. "Counselor?"

"If it pleases the court, I'd like to call Lieutenant Maria Hall back to the stand."

"I object, Your Honor," the government lawyer spat out. "Her testimony is highly prejudicial and obviously biased."

James' lawyer chuckled and shook his head. "We've already established that the lieutenant is an expert in the matter of high-level criminals. In fact, my esteemed colleague is the one who established that. I don't think it's wrong to ask her opinion about this desert showdown."

The judge nodded. "I'll allow it. I think I know how to filter out bias, counselor."

The lieutenant headed back to the stand and was sworn in again.

James' lawyer walked over to her with a smile. He nodded at the other lawyer.

"So, he maintains that Mr. Brownstone lured a man out to have a duel with him and that it's cold-blooded murder, but according to the official report, Mr. Brownstone, despite being ambushed, was still offering people a chance to surrender, and even offered this vicious Lars Hansen a chance to survive." He lifted a transcript he held in his hand. "If I may quote Mr. Brownstone, 'You're not leaving here, Lars. I might not kill you, but I'm gonna break your legs at least. Then I'll call AET and have them pick you up.

I'm sure the cops would love to send your *expletive* to an ultra-max for what you did in Atlanta."

The lieutenant nodded. "That's accurate, and matches with the footage of the fight the department recovered, even if not all of it was shown in court."

"How would you parse those last few statements in the context of what you know about James Brownstone?"

The lieutenant shrugged. "Clearly, Brownstone wasn't just out to kill the man, and I should also note that the other counsel neglected to show the portion of the fight where Mr. Brownstone disabled men and refused to kill them, but Lars Hansen did. That's the kind of man Lars Hansen was."

A murmur rippled through the crowd. Davis scribbled some notes at his table.

"And as for Atlanta…" The AET officer locked eyes with James, her next words coming out deliberate and slow. "Lars Hansen killed an entire AET team in Atlanta. Not just that, he's killed many innocent civilians. What do you think James Brownstone was supposed to do to stop Lars Hansen? Sit down and have tea and crumpets with him? Challenge him to bowling?" She let out a bitter laugh. "The guy even stupidly risked his own life to drag Hansen all the way out to the Salton Sea so not *one* innocent person was at risk. Yes, he lured the man in a sense, but taking advantage of a dangerous criminal's arrogance to make sure that no one else gets hurt sounds like something we should be applauding, not punishing, unless we want major showdowns with enhanced criminals to occur in downtown LA."

James grunted. It was nice to be understood, but he

wished Hall had understood earlier, if only because she might have spoken to Shay on his behalf.

Silverberg nodded. "Be that as it may, Lieutenant, even if he's a good man who takes down criminals, he's still in a dangerous line of work. I think the state would say that's not something a young girl should be exposed to. What are your thoughts on that?"

The other lawyer shot up. "Objection. Irrelevant and prejudicial. Lieutenant Hall is not a child psychologist, and not qualified to testify on how Mr. Brownstone's lifestyle choices might affect Alice Anderson."

"Alison Brownstone," the girl muttered under her breath.

James' lawyer laughed. "Your Honor, with all due respect, the state's whole argument is that Mr. Brownstone is a dangerous man who is unfit to be an adoptive parent because of his profession. I think the input of a police officer in a particularly dangerous line of police work is relevant."

The judged nodded. "I'll allow it."

Alison muttered a few choice things about Davis' parentage under her breath. James resisted a chuckle.

The lieutenant grinned with a feral intensity. "Should I be allowed to adopt a kid?"

Silverberg shrugged. "I don't know, Lieutenant. Should you?"

She pointed to Sergeant Mack. "Should he? He's a cop. It's dangerous. I'm AET. It's very dangerous. Should anyone in the military be allowed to? Should firefighters? I read an article the other day that talked about how dangerous being a commercial fisherman is, especially with all the sea monsters in the oceans these days. No fishermen allowed to adopt kids? Is that the kind of society we have now? We going to tell people who risk their lives that they aren't good enough to take care of kids?"

James' lawyer nodded quickly. "That's a good point." He shrugged. "I don't know. If we establish here that simply being in a dangerous line of work means you're not a good parent, I guess the state's going to have to take a lot of kids away from their parents."

The other lawyer glared at him. "Objection. Inflammatory, irrelevant, and prejudicial."

The judge shot a warning glance at the first lawyer. "Let's keep things focused on Mr. Brownstone and Alison Anderson, counselor. Don't make me remind you again."

"I apologize, your honor." Silverberg shrugged. "I've no further questions for Lieutenant Hall, unless my esteemed colleague wants to talk with her?"

The government lawyer shook his head.

The judge picked up his gavel. "Lieutenant, you're dismissed. We'll have a ten-minute recess before continuing." He banged the gavel.

Alison stood and stretched. "I'm going to go get a drink. I'll be right back."

James nodded. "You need any help?"

"Nope. I'm good. Just need some air before I do something I regret to that scumbag lawyer."

James chuckled. "I know how you feel."

Alison waved and joined the flow of people leaving the courtroom.

Shay leaned from the front row of the gallery toward James. "What the fuck was up with you offering them a chance to surrender, especially after that ambush shit? It's bad enough that you went out to the desert and got yourself ambushed, but it's beyond fucking moronic that you tried to play nice after that."

James shrugged. "I knew I was being taped," he whispered back. "I couldn't have everyone thinking I waste people without remorse, even though I mostly do. Lucky I did, otherwise that government lawyer would be going to town on me even more."

Shay snorted. "You're lucky it worked out for you. Next time, kill them like you're ready to get back in bed and they are making you late."

Silverberg returned to the table after a quick chat with the judge and smiled. "Things are going well, I think."

James shrugged. "If you say so."

The other man chuckled. "Trust me, barring any sort of weird surprises, I'm confident we'll win."

Weird surprises? James was an alien bounty hunter trying to adopt a half-Drow girl. His whole life was one giant weird surprise.

Fifteen minutes later, James was annoyed by something that *wasn't* a surprise. His lawyer had told him to expect a long list of statements about what a mercenary scumbag he was, but hearing them read aloud in the nasal voice of the court clerk annoyed the ever-living fuck out of him.

The court clerk cleared her throat as she read off another statement. "I don't get out of bed for less than a level three. Not worth the money. I'm not a charity." She moved down to the next one a second later. "I'm not a Good Samaritan. I'm a bounty hunter, and I get paid. Come up with some cash, and maybe I'll look into it. Otherwise, I don't give an *expletive*."

Davis nodded. "Thank you. Your Honor, let the record reflect that all of those were taken from sworn statements by people interviewed by our office concerning James Brownstone's attitude. I've also submitted into evidence several supplementary documents that contain even more sworn statements concerning Mr. Brownstone's attitude toward money, and how it's obvious that money, and not a concern for law and order, motivates him."

"Duly noted," the judge responded.

Alison rolled her eyes and leaned over to whisper. "Oh, because it's so wrong to get paid for your job? Not like that jerk is working for free."

The judge looked at James' lawyer. "Counselor?"

Silverberg smiled. "At this time, I'd like to call Detective West of the Las Vegas Metropolitan Police Department as a rebuttal witness."

The detective was soon at the witness stand and sworn in. He looked comfortable and poised.

James' lawyer sighed. "So, that's a pretty damning list of people claiming that Mr. Brownstone is a scumbag who doesn't care about anything but money, don't you think?"

"Objection," Davis shouted. "Leading the witness."

The judge nodded. "Counselor, ask questions, don't testify yourself. I won't warn you again."

Silverberg gave a little apologetic shrug. "Of course, Your Honor." He turned back toward the detective. "You recently had occasion to work with Mr. Brownstone during the investigation into an enhanced serial killer, the so-called Red-Eyes Killer, in Las Vegas, correct?"

The cop nodded. "That is correct. Detective Lafayette and I." He pointed toward his partner in the gallery.

Silverberg nodded slowly. "And did you have any occasion to discuss Mr. Brownstone's motivation for pursuing the Red Eyes Killer?"

"Yes, I did, as did my partner."

The other lawyer frowned. "Objection. Hearsay."

James' lawyer grinned like a hungry shark. "Were you

present at this conversation that Mr. Brownstone had with your partner? That is, did you personally overhear everything said by Mr. Brownstone and your partner."

The cop nodded toward Detective Lafayette in the gallery. "Yes."

The judge pounded his gavel. "Objection overruled."

Davis sighed and shook his head.

Silverberg gestured toward James. "Please tell us about any conversations you had with Mr. Brownstone about his motivations for pursuing the killer. Anything that would give us insight into whether money is his sole motivating factor."

"Of course." The cop took a deep breath. "The thing you need to keep in mind is that the Red-Eyes Killer was murdering parents in front of young children. That monster was creating orphans, and Brownstone's an orphan. I believe that he was—"

The government lawyer shot up. "Objection. Supposition."

The judge slammed his gavel. "Sustained. I must direct you, Detective, to testify only to what you have directly seen and heard. You know better than to testify to the state of mind of someone else."

Detective West frowned. "Yes, Your Honor. Anyway, Brownstone met with the daughter of the first victim. He was visibly upset by it. He made it very clear in later statements that he wanted to make sure this killer was taken down. Because of the difficulty of dealing with an enhanced threat, discussion of the necessity of potentially killing the Red-Eyes Killer came up, and you have to remember, at the time, the bounty wasn't dead-or-alive.

Brownstone seemed more concerned with ending the threat than the money." He shrugged. "And he's not even a Vegas man. He told me he'd come to Vegas just to get some barbeque at Jessie Rae's. Great place, by the way."

Silverberg chuckled. "I'm sure it is, but what you're saying is that James Brownstone got involved in tracking down a serial killer when he didn't have to, and even though he knew it might end in an altercation ending with him making little to no money."

"Yes, that would be an accurate summary of what I witnessed. He's also continued to be useful in Las Vegas in terms of bounty hunting."

The lawyer's face grew grave. "But isn't it true that you can't normally afford to hire someone of Brownstone's skill? You had to get special funding to put a bounty on the Red-Eyes Killer according to your signed statements submitted into evidence."

"That's true, but it's also true that we negotiated with Mr. Brownstone to have bounty hunters from his agency work on some critical bounties for the city of Las Vegas. These are all lower-level bounties, but Brownstone still cares about them being taken care of. It's not like he needed to take guys from Los Angeles and send them to Vegas. I mean, if you think about..." He turned to the judge. "I'm not saying I know what's going through Brownstone's head, but it costs money to maintain office space in Las Vegas, then there's gas, and those guys aren't available for Los Angeles. Lot more bounties in LA too, so if anything, it seems like Brownstone's not making as much money as he could by helping Vegas out."

Davis frowned at his table. It looked like he was going to say something, but he kept his mouth shut.

Silverberg glanced the other lawyer's way for a second as if daring him to object. "That's interesting, Detective. Is this help from the Brownstone Agency of *that* much use to the city of Las Vegas? I mean, just a few men cleaning up a few bounties here and there can't be that big of a deal, right?"

The detective laughed. "His team has already cleaned up twenty percent of the backlog of bounties in our city."

Several excited murmurs broke out among the people in the gallery. Several reporters furiously scribbled in their pads, their phones not allowed to be on by the judge's order.

The lawyer scratched his cheek. "Interesting. Very interesting. And do you see any of these bounty hunters here today?"

The detective pointed to Trey and several of the others. "Mr. Garfield and several of his team members are over there, of course."

"Let the record reflect, Your Honor, that the detective is pointing to the men my esteemed colleague complained about being dangerous criminals and gang members earlier."

The judge nodded. "Duly noted."

Detective West smiled. "They've been a great help. I don't personally work with them much because I'm not involved in bounty processing, but Sergeant Choi has submitted a statement about them."

"Yes, I submitted that statement into evidence earlier. So it is your professional opinion, then, that your relationship with James Brownstone, both direct and indirect, has made the city of Las Vegas a safer place?"

"Certainly." The detective locked eyes with Davis. "And anyone who says otherwise is snorting too much dust."

Scattered laughter broke out in the gallery.

James enjoyed the look of defeat on Davis' face. Detective Lafayette's testimony following his partner's further wounded the ruthless mercenary theory the government lawyer had been pushing. Hell, even the bounty hunter was impressed by the cops' stressing that he didn't care about money.

In truth, it wasn't as if Davis were completely wrong. James *did* sometimes take on jobs for something other than money, but he was still far from a do-gooder. He'd destroyed the Harriken because they wouldn't leave him alone, and he'd helped take down the Nuevo Gulf Cartel because it was a threat to Shay, not because he couldn't stand the existence of criminals.

Red Eyes was different. He'd taken down that monster as a father representing a daughter who had not been strong enough to do it herself. Maybe that was a type of selflessness to some, but he figured it was more straight vengeance. Not exactly the kind of thing Father McCartney would encourage at church.

The government lawyer sat at his table for a moment, his face in his hands. Someone slipped in from outside the courtroom and hurried through the gallery until he was right behind the lawyer. He leaned in to whisper to Davis.

The lawyer's face brightened, and his smug grin returned.

What the fuck is he so happy for?

The judge frowned. "Something you need to share with the court, counselor?"

Davis nodded. "Your Honor, I request a sidebar."

"Very well. Mr. Silverberg, please join us."

The two lawyers walked over to the judge. Davis started speaking quietly and gesticulating wildly. Silverberg frowned and shook his head, clearly upset by something. He pointed toward the doors several times.

Alison and James exchanged looks, but neither said anything. Until they knew what was going on, it'd be pointless to worry.

Several minutes of discussion between the lawyers and the judge followed before the two lawyers headed back to their tables and sat. The judge motioned the court clerk over and whispered something to him.

Silverberg sighed and shook his head. "This might get ugly, but I have to warn you, James. No matter what happens, keep your cool. We can still win this, I promise you."

The bounty hunter blinked and looked at Davis. "What the hell?"

What trick does that asshole have up his sleeve now?

Alison reached over to squeeze James' hand, and he gave hers a comforting squeeze back.

The judge cleared his throat. "We have…an unusual request, but this is an unusual situation. Let the record reflect that Her Royal Highness Laena, Queen of the Drow of Oriceran, has requested entry into the proceedings. She will be testifying as an expert on Drow."

Alison gasped.

The gallery erupted into a din. The judge slammed his gavel down several times until people quieted.

James snorted. "At least she asked."

Silverberg shook his head and frowned.

Yev's face scrunched so much that James wondered if he'd developed spontaneous kidney stones. A regal-looking elf next to him whom James didn't recognize didn't look any happier.

Who's that, Yev's boss?

The judge banged his gavel. "We'll take a small recess to prepare for the logistics of this matter."

Silverberg frowned. "They're going to try and push the idea that the girl belongs with her own people. They are going to say a lot of things that might upset you."

"I'm her people," James rumbled. "And this whole hearing upsets me."

The lawyer nodded. "If this were a normal proceeding I'd get this tossed right out, especially this late in the game, but the Oriceran connection changes everything. Nothing about this case has been normal, and now I understand why."

James grunted. "Yeah, at least now we know who's been behind all this shit. The same fuckers who keep trying to kill me."

Alison swallowed and bit her lip. "You don't think she'd

try anything, do you, Dad? And if she does…do you have *it* with you?"

The bounty hunter almost laughed. Bonding with the amulet and taking on a Drow queen in the middle of a courthouse would be ballsy even by his standards. He didn't want to risk it, not when Alison and so many other innocent people could get hurt.

Neither he nor Shay were armed and the cops present had only small handguns, not the armor, arms, and magical equipment AET would need to take on a Drow. Still, he needed to make sure Alison was comfortable.

James patted his chest where his amulet hung, separated from his skin by a thin piece of metal. "Let's hope it doesn't come to that." He glanced over his shoulder. "Okay, I've got to hit the head before the woman who kept sending people to kill me shows up. Wouldn't want to have to go in the middle of a fight."

Alison rolled her eyes, and Silverberg chuckled.

James smiled at Alison. "I'll be right back, kid. You stay here. " He inclined his head toward Yev and the elf beside him. "I'm guessing that as long as they're around, the queen won't try to snatch you."

"Okay, Dad." Alison took a deep breath and slowly let it out.

The bounty hunter stood and made his way toward the back.

Fucking Drow. Why can't you just leave us the fuck alone?

A few minutes later, Silverberg gave the girl a smile. "It'll be okay. This is just more testimony. This isn't as simple as Drow demanding custody. This is still America, and you were born here, not on Oriceran." He chuckled. "That said, Alison, we're in uncharted waters and probably about to help establish precedent."

"I don't care to be honest. I just want to stay with my dad."

"I understand, and I'm doing everything I can to make that happen."

Alison turned toward the gallery. "What do you think, Aunt…" She frowned.

Shay was nowhere to be found. It didn't seem like her to just up and leave without saying anything.

Alison turned toward Silverberg. "Did you see where Shay went?"

The man shook his head. "Sorry, Alison. I'm sure she'll be back before the recess is over."

Just as the lawyer said that James pushed back into the courtroom and made his way back to the table. Shay popped back into the room a few seconds later and went to the gallery.

"Where did you go?" Alison asked.

"Was just talking with Peyton about who on the human side of things was responsible for this mess." A dark grin appeared on her face. "We've almost narrowed it down, but it might be a few more days before we can figure it out."

Alison was just about to ask another question when she gasped. One of the most powerful yet twisted souls she'd ever seen strode through the door. Laena. Drow flanked their queen.

"It's her," she whispered.

James sighed. "Yeah. Damn it."

Shay sneered. "We all owe that bitch a punch or three."

"So much anger, so much hatred." Alison shivered and wrapped her arms around her shoulders. "I've never seen anything like it, even from…" She sighed and shook her head.

James frowned. "It'll be all right, kid. I promise. No matter what it takes, it'll be all right."

Alison leaned forward to whisper into his ear. "Use the wish if you have to."

James nodded slowly. Most people present reflexively stood as the queen strode forward, but Shay, James, and Alison remained seated. There was no way they'd grant that woman any respect. Silverberg also remained seated.

The queen's guards peeled off and moved to stand along the wall on either side of the room.

"Interesting," Laena murmured, her voice accented in an odd way that seemed exotic but was not easily pinned to any Earth accent.

Davis hurried over and bowed, of all things. Alison rolled her eyes, and James grunted his disapproval.

"Your Highness, if you'd just go to the witness stand." The lawyer gestured in that direction. "And we'll swear you in once the proceedings get started."

The queen all but glided to the stand, turning to face Alison as she sat, laying one hand over another. Swirling eddies of negative energy wrapped around her soul, the sight almost making Alison nauseated.

The court clerk moved forward. "All rise. Court is in session, the Honorable John Matthews presiding."

Everyone in the courtroom stood except Laena.

Alison sighed at the flashes of fear spiking through the clerk's soul. What kind of woman inspired that kind of fear?

Was it just her power? Two of the Light Elves in the room felt as if they held something near that kind of power, but the girl honestly wondered if the queen could kill everyone in the room except her dad.

The only thing Alison could be sure of was that no matter what happened, she didn't want to leave LA to go with that woman.

You're a monster, Laena. I've read all about you Drow, and I want nothing to do with you.

The judge moved to the bench and sat. "You may be seated."

Everyone complied.

The court clerk walked over to Laena and lifted her right hand. "Your Highness, please raise your right hand."

The queen complied.

"Do you swear to tell the truth, the whole truth, so help you, God?"

Laena snorted. "I have no need to tell falsehoods, but I don't recognize your human god."

James muttered something under his breath.

The court clerk looked at the judge. He nodded back, and the court clerk moved away from the witness stand. Laena, Queen of the Drow, was about to testify in a California family court.

James stared at the Drow queen, the sight strange given the context—an ancient elven queen sitting in a witness stand. Her dark skin and the deep blue of her elegant and elaborate gown contrasted with her bright white hair.

Everything about her screamed regal, but also dangerous. Her slightest movement spoke of confidence and power. Even the bounty hunter found himself twitching a little and aching to bond with his amulet just in case she decided she wanted to make trouble.

Why do I get the feeling she could kick the asses of those three Drow who went after me?

He glanced at Alison. The girl's gaze had been locked on the queen since her arrival, and her frown had been stuck on her face for nearly as long.

What do you see, Alison? Whatever it is, you don't like it. I can tell that much.

The bounty hunter took small, controlled breaths, hoping nothing violent happened. Protecting Alison would have to come first, even if it meant becoming the vicious killer the government lawyer kept accusing him of being.

He'd also seen what Drow could do, and he didn't want a roomful of people to be cut down by some crazed elf.

Davis cleared his throat. "Your Highness, we're here today to settle the matter of James Brownstone's adoption of Alison Anderson. While it's the state's primary contention that he's an unfit guardian, her status as a half-Drow also leads us to believe that she would be better off with her own people, and we wanted to explore that with you."

The queen gave a curt nod. "I agree. The Drow are an ancient and proud race. Her magical potential cannot be maximized under the guidance of that thuggish bounty hunter."

James snorted.

I'll show you thug.

She smirked at him. "And that is an important point to realize—the difference between humans and Oricerans. An Oriceran, especially a Drow, is a magical being. It's misleading to simply look at the similar shapes some of us have and not accept how important magic is to the essence of our very souls."

Davis nodded. "On Oriceran, if someone were half-Drow, what would happen?"

Silverberg stood. "Objection, Your Honor. We're in the United States of America on Earth, not some Drow Kingdom on Oriceran. Drow customs and laws hold no sway here."

Davis shook his head. "*United Nut Company vs. the Thirty-Second Willen Collective* clearly established that

Oriceran customs must be taken into account when evaluating reasonable reactions from Oriceran citizens."

The judge nodded. "I'll allow it."

The queen smiled, although there was something unsettling and hungry about it. "On Oriceran, unions resulting in half-Drow are quite rare, but the parties involved would normally understand that it would be better for a partial Drow child to be with the Drow people because of our unique magical and cultural needs. Even Light Elves would agree." Her voice dripped contempt as she glanced at Yev.

Davis followed her gaze. "Of course, of course. Another question. Are mothers important in Drow culture?"

"Extremely so. It would be one thing if her mother were still alive to help raise her, but the idea of this single male human raising a Drow girl is, from our perspective, completely absurd." She shook her head. "It would be like… you giving a human child to be raised by one of your monkeys. The creature might manage to raise the child without killing her, but she'd not grow into her capacity, and she'd meet only a fraction of her true potential."

If I was a monkey, I'd be throwing some shit at you about now, bitch.

James frowned and Alison squeezed his hand, even as she kept her attention focused on the queen.

The government lawyer glanced at the judge and the queen. "Your Highness, we're still getting used to magic on Earth. As an expert on magic, could you give us some insight into the dangers of uncontrolled magic, and how Alison might have to deal with that issue?"

The bounty hunter allowed himself a smile. Davis had

screwed up with that line of questioning. Judging by the huge smile on Silverberg's face, he'd realized it too.

Laena let out a grim laugh. "Oh, I think I need to explain the dangers of uncontrolled magic. Your poor planet has already experienced it. The presence of men like Brownstone—" she flicked her wrist in her direction—"already proves what it's like. If young Alison isn't properly trained, she'll never learn how to properly control her magic, and Drow blood is powerful. She'll become a threat to herself and others, and even if she's not trying, she risks hurting people."

Worried chatter filled the room, and the judge banged his gavel until it quieted.

The queen let out a long sigh. "I don't say this to make you fear the girl. I'm sure she is a sweet girl who has suffered far too much, but it's important for humans to realize that magical Oricerans aren't just humans with a few differences in appearance. Our fundamental essence is different, and that should never be forgotten." Her face twitched as if she were doing her best to hold back a sneer.

Fuck you. I'm not human, and I've been doing all right by Alison. Meanwhile, all you assholes have been doing is sending people to kill me. Alison's mother left you for a reason, and I have a pretty good idea what it was.

You'll have to take my fucking head off before I let you leave with Alison. I don't give a shit what the court says or what you do on Oriceran.

Davis gave James a cool look before turning back to the queen. "Is there anything else you want to add, Your Highness?"

She nodded. "Yes. I appreciate Mr. Brownstone's efforts

thus far, and if he truly cares for this girl, he'll release her into the custody of her people so that we can help her grow to the maximum of her ability rather than being selfish."

"Thank you, Queen Laena." The government lawyer turned to the judge. "That's all I have, Your Honor."

The judged nodded to James' lawyer. "Counselor?"

Silverberg stood and clucked his tongue as he made his way over toward the witness stand. "So, because she's half-Drow, Your Highness, she's all Drow? Is that what you're saying?"

"It's simply that she's better served with our people, and yes, being part Drow does mean she's effectively all Drow."

The lawyer looked at the judge. "That sounds like the one-drop rule to me. Lots of nastiness in American history because of that kind of thinking. The last place I expected to hear it is in an American courtroom in this century. Guess we're more advanced than Oriceran in ways other than technology."

Davis slammed a hand on the table. "Objection. Highly inflammatory."

The judge banged his gavel. "Sustained. Mr. Silverberg, keep your questions and comments contained."

"Of course. Of course." The lawyer turned back to the queen. "My point is the girl is half-human. You don't think humans can raise her?"

Laena snorted. "From what I understand, the human half didn't want her."

"James Brownstone does. That's the beauty of adoption, Your Highness."

Her eyes narrowed. "Desire is insufficient. Ignoring the fundamental difference between a Drow and a human is idealistic at best, foolish and ignorant at worst. Good intentions don't always make for a better world."

"Perhaps. So, before you showed up, there was a lot of time spent establishing how dangerous James Brownstone is."

She shrugged. "That only suggests more reasons why the girl should be with the Drow."

"The danger of James Brownstone?"

"Yes."

Silverberg chuckled. He moved back to his table and grabbed a piece of paper. He handed it to the court clerk, who handed it to the judge.

"I'm entering into evidence a report from the LAPD AET detailing a recent battle with three enhanced threats in the Salton Sea. Specifically, three Drow warriors.

Laena shook her head. "Such arrogance."

"Do you deny that these Drow attacked James Brownstone and the AET?"

The queen took a deep breath and slowly let it out. "Humans kill a lot of people. Do you ask your king to keep track of them all?"

"This is America, Your Highness. We don't serve a king. We elect a president." Silverberg nodded toward his briefcase on his table. "I can show you pictures of the aftermath and some of the helmet footage from the police if you like. These Drow were vicious and powerful, and even after near-defeat, it looked like they planned to take everyone with them—some sort of final self-sacrifice magic that opened a portal to another world." He sucked in a breath. "Quite frankly, say what you will about James Brownstone, but as best as I can tell, even Davis over there isn't claiming he'd send a pile of people into another world when they beat him in a fight."

Laena slapped her hand on the armrest, the sound echoing. "The Drow are strong. I will not apologize for that." She smirked. "Because humans are weak, I should be saddened? Because your AET can't handle us?"

"So Drow are strong?"

"Yes."

"And you have no problem with them hurting others?"

The queen pointed at James. "He hurts others in defense of your human order. If a Drow must cause pain for the strength of our people, who I am to question it any more than you would question James Brownstone or your AET?"

Silverberg leaned forward. "Would you call yourself a warrior race?"

Laena scoffed. "Of course we are. A true warrior race, unlike your pathetic kind."

He locked eyes with the Drow queen. "Would you say the average Drow is dangerous?"

"Of course we are." She sniffed. "We are Drow. That should be enough to convince you that that girl belongs with us. You won't be able to handle her."

Silverberg looked over his shoulder at Alison and then back at the queen. "Because she's half-Drow?"

"It's more than enough to defeat weak humans."

"Well, James Brownstone already defeated three of your warriors, so it seems to me he can handle one half-Drow girl."

Laena shot of the seat, her eyes blazing with fury. "How dare you, human? I should burn this courtroom to ashes because of your insolence. You mock the Drow? You mock *me?*"

The judge banged his gavel. "Order. There will be order."

The cops present, along with the courtroom police officer, all tensed, their hands lowering toward their weapons.

James frowned and rose, reaching inside his jacket in case he needed to bond with his amulet. The two Drow near the walls exchanged glances and hurried toward the queen.

"Your Highness, please calm down," one called urgently. Another looked at Yev and the Light Elf next to him, both of whom stood now with frowns on their faces.

The judge continued banging his gavel. "Your Highness, if you do not calm down, I'll be forced to have you removed."

The queen snickered, then looked at Yev and the other elf. "Fine, but I'm done with these absurd questions."

The judge swallowed and nodded. "The witness is dismissed."

Laena stomped out of the witness stand, glaring at James Brownstone as she strode toward the gallery.

Davis sat at his table, rubbing his temples.

James sat back down and let his hand drop, offering a grateful nod toward the Light Elves. He suspected that, without their presence, the queen would have started killing people.

Alison shook her head. "What a nutjob," she whispered.

The judge cleared this throat. "We shall take a short recess so everyone's tempers can calm, and at that point, unless they are any other surprise witnesses, it will be time to hear from Alison Anderson."

Alison bit her lip and looked at James.

He smiled at her. "Just tell them the truth. The rest will work itself out."

James frowned a few minutes later as Alison was sworn in on the stand, a slight look of panic on her face. He would have preferred it if Laena were absent entirely, but the smirking Drow queen remained in the courtroom.

You lasted, what, five minutes pretending not to be an evil bitch?

Silverberg approached Alison with a smile. "Don't worry. This will all be over soon enough. Just wanted to ask you a few questions, and then the judge can decide what's going to happen. All you have to do is answer openly and honestly. Don't worry about what anyone is thinking or what they expect to hear."

She nodded. "Okay, I do can that."

"So, Alison, tell us a little about yourself."

"Like what?"

"What kinds of things do you like?"

Alison blushed. "Lots of things."

"Such as?"

"My friends, and you know…boys."

James gritted his teeth, annoyed to hear that despite the situation. Scattered laughs came from other people in the courtroom. Maybe it was petty to care about boys hitting on his daughter, but it was those small fatherly thoughts that kept him grounded and in control.

Silverberg nodded slowly. "Boys. Hmm, sounds a lot like any other normal teenager." He glanced at James. "Do you think James Brownstone understands you?"

Alison laughed. "He does okay. What dad *really* understands a teenage girl, though?"

More laughter followed.

The lawyer smiled. "What dad, indeed? I'd like to hear a little bit more about your background before you lost your parents. It's my understanding that you didn't go to school then."

"Yeah, that's true." The girl sighed.

"Why, Alison?"

Alison took several deep breaths. "Because…I can't really see. I'm blind." She ignored the murmurs and kept speaking. "I can see souls and energies of living things and magic, but I can't see like a normal person, so I've always felt like a freak. I didn't want to go to regular school and have people ask me about it, tease me, or bully me."

"And what about now? Do you go to school now?"

"Yes, I go to a government magic school in Virginia." Alison smiled.

The lawyer glanced at the Drow queen with a faint smile on his face. "A government magic school? So there are witches, wizards, and elves there? Those sort of people, teaching you how to use your powers?"

Laena's frown deepened.

The girl nodded. "It's a safe place to learn how to use my magic, and there are a diverse group of students there, not just one race. I have great friends there, and I'm not coddled like a spoiled princess. I've grown a lot since going there."

"Sounds like a great environment." Silverberg glanced at Davis as if waiting for the other lawyer to object, but the man said nothing. "Good, good. So, tell me about James Brownstone."

She shrugged. "What's to tell? I love him, and I already consider him my dad, no matter what this court says."

More than a few audible sighs and sniffles sounded in the room, including from a few Oricerans.

"But the state says he's a dangerous and vicious man, practically a criminal. Does it scare you to be around a man like that? A dangerous bounty hunter who has been involved in so many dangerous battles?"

Alison shook her head. "No. I'm scared for *him* some-times, but never for myself."

"I see. And how does James Brownstone make you feel?"

She offered the bounty hunter a warm smile. "Safe. I always know that if he's around, nothing bad will ever happen to me. He won't let it."

James smiled back, some of the tension and concern even over the Drow queen fading. They could do this. They could win. All the character assassination and dirty tricks by the government lawyer wouldn't matter if Alison made her feelings clear to the judge.

Silverberg leaned forward. "I've got one final question for you, Alison. Who do you want to be with?"

The girl locked gazes with the queen, letting defiance settle over her face. "Family isn't about blood. Family is about the people who actually care. James Brownstone is my dad, and he always will be, no matter what anybody says."

The lawyer looked up at the judge. "That's all I have, Your Honor."

The judge looked at Davis. "Counselor?"

The government lawyer shook his head. "I have no questions at this time."

The judge raised his gavel. "Very well, then. There will be a short recess while I consider all the information and make my decision." He banged his gavel. "Court is adjourned."

Alison and the lawyer made their way back over to James' table.

James let out a long, slow breath. "Did we win?"

The lawyer smiled. "I have a good feeling about this, James, especially after the rant of Her Royal Highness. The way Davis has clammed up as well proves that the jig is up, and he doesn't want to be seen as using the power of our government to do the bidding of psychotic Oriceran queens who think they are better than humans."

"Good. I'd hate to have to make a scene." James grinned.

"She made enough of a scene for the both of you."

Alison pulled James into an embrace. Shay smiled.

The three sat there chatting quietly about what kinds of

places they might want to go to on vacation for ten minutes before the judge returned.

Everyone looked his way, surprised at his quick return.

"Damn it." Silverberg winced. "That was too quick."

James frowned. "What do you mean?"

"Too damned quick." The lawyer scrubbed a hand down his face. "I'm so sorry, James."

Alison shook her head. "No, it can't be."

Shay gritted her teeth.

The court clerk stood. "All rise. Court is in session, the Honorable John Matthews presiding."

Everyone stood except for Laena. She frowned, her arms crossed.

The judge sat. "Please be seated." He looked between the two tables. "I'm sure you're surprised by how quickly I came back, but with all the evidence presented as well as the testimony presented, the decision is easy." He took a deep breath.

Everyone fell silent, few even daring to breathe as they awaited his decision.

"This court hereby rules that the state's petition to block the adoption of Alison Anderson by James Brownstone is denied. The adoption will proceed."

Alison shot out of her chair, gasping.

James blinked several times, unsure he could believe what he was hearing. Half the room cheered while James and Alison embraced.

The queen stood, her lips curled into a sneer, and walked toward James' table.

"Brownstone," Laena hissed. "Your name shall be a

curse among our people for generations. Drow will spit on the ground at its mere mention."

The bounty hunter released Alison and turned to face the queen. He wasn't bonded with his amulet, but he wasn't about to let her intimidate him.

Several of the police officers stood, their hands on their guns.

James shook his head at them, as did Lieutenant Hall. They'd both seen a Drow in action. It'd be a slaughter if anyone tried something.

Laena stalked forward. "Brownstone, who arranged for some of my strongest warriors to die. Brownstone, who has taken something that isn't his. Your name vexes me, and here I am expected to abide by the laws of some country of backward barbarians on this backward savage planet? I will not stand for it."

"Queen Laena," Yev called from the gallery. "Don't compound the situation with any unnecessary actions. I'd ask you return to Oriceran."

The Drow Queen sneered and didn't even look his way. "Fine. For now, I'll recognize the authority of the barbarian court. She extended her hand and smiled. "They say on Earth that you can tell a lot about a man by his handshake. Let's see what I can tell about you, James Brownstone."

James shrugged and extended his hand. "Glad to see you can be reasonable. I promise you I'll take good care of her."

She grabbed his hand, and a pulse of black surrounded her hand.

A wave of nausea and pain shot into James, and he fell to his knees, the room spinning around him.

Laena laughed. "Impressive. Even that mild death touch would have killed the average human."

"On the ground," shouted Sergeant Mack, his gun out. "You're under arrest."

The cops all slowly advanced on the queen. Her two guards sprang to her side, shadow blades forming in their hands and a black nimbus surrounding them.

James groaned and pushed to his feet, feeling weak. Shay and Alison rushed over to catch him before he fell to the ground again. Shay pulled one of James' healing potion out of her pocket and uncorked it.

"Open up," she commanded. "Glad I thought to bring this, just in case."

Alison eyed Laena as the Drow queen watched James, disgust in her eyes.

The bounty hunter managed to open his mouth, and Shay emptied the potion into it.

"I'm tired of being humiliated by humans," Laena shouted. "You will all die before my power. Your blood will be the payment for your arrogance." She raised her hand and blasted a small black orb toward James.

Alison jumped in front of it, and the queen's eyes widened as the girl carved through the black orb with a hand enveloped in purple energy. Laena fired another blast, and Alison slashed through it again, dissipating it to nothingness.

James shook his head, trying to concentrate. The pain and nausea were starting to fade.

A complex melody rang out, and a column of translucent white energy surrounded the Drow. Yev and the elf beside him advanced toward the Dark Elves, frowns on their faces.

"Do you wish war, Laena?" Yev shouted. "You will stop this madness."

"You dare speak to me that way?" The queen sneered. "You think you can hold me, Light Elf? I'll destroy any who stand in the way of the Drow."

The elf standing beside Yev shook his head. "We know we can't hold you for long, but we don't have to."

A few quick motions of their hands accompanied another melody. A bright portal winked into existence right behind them, and the column disappeared in a bright flash, the Drow yelling as they tumbled into the portal.

Laena managed to get in one last glare at James before the portal winked out of existence, leaving a room full of angry police and confused onlookers.

Another portal opened, and the Light Elves stepped through, grim-faced.

Alison spun back toward James. "Dad, you okay?"

The bounty hunter looked far less gray than he had a minute before, and he didn't need Shay's help to stand anymore. He nodded slowly.

Fuck. That bitch got me good.

"Not my finest hour, but I'll live," he rumbled.

Lieutenant Hall and Sergeant Mack hurried over to him.

The AET officer frowned. "So that's the bitch who almost got my men killed twice."

"Are those other elves arresting her?" Sergeant Mack asked. "Is that what happened?"

Shay shook her head. "No. They just sent her back to Oriceran, I think."

James shrugged. "She's gone for now, and soon Alison will legally be my daughter." He shook his head. "I don't give two fu…flips about the Drow queen right now. Let's get the hell out of here and celebrate."

Lieutenant Hall smiled. "I know just the place."

2 2

An hour later, James found himself at about the last place he ever expected to celebrate his victory—the Black Sun. He sat at a table with Lieutenant Hall, Sergeant Mack, Alison, and Shay. The cop-to-criminal ratio was high that night, and even the criminals seemed in an unusually good mood, with many stopping by to pat him on the shoulder and congratulate him on his victory.

It's weird to have people act all nice to me instead of being afraid of me. Not sure if I like it.

Lieutenant Hall chuckled and shook her head as Tyler set down a few new bottles of beer and a Coke for Alison. The only person who looked uncomfortable with the situation was the information broker. His gaze kept cutting to James as if he expected the bounty hunter to go berserk at any second and throw someone through the front door.

James looked up at the other man and shrugged. "I won today. Just here to celebrate. I don't blame you for them having the Hansen footage. I know it got seized by cops."

"Not AET," Lieutenant Hall mumbled.

Tyler chuckled and shook his head. "A waitress called in sick. I've got to hit the tables. I'll be back in a few minutes."

Alison took a sip of her drink. "What about the Drow queen? What if she comes back? She's such an obsessive and bitchy nutjob, I can't imagine she'll just give up."

James grunted. "Don't worry. I think the Light Elves are going to keep her under control for now. I've got a few ideas on how to handle it after that." He glanced at Shay, who gave him a quick nod back.

She was looking into some things for him, including a few artifacts that might be useful for delivering a message to Laena.

Lieutenant Hall extended her hand to James. "I never did apologize for being a complete bitch to you, Brownstone, but I hope what I did in court can at least somewhat make up for that. Bygones, and all that."

He shook her hand. "It meant a lot. I wouldn't call myself a jaguar, but…" He shrugged.

She snorted. "Calling you a shit-throwing monkey just doesn't sound as intimidating."

Shay laughed, and Alison spat some of her drink through her nose.

Mack clapped James on the back. "You sure you're okay to be out partying? Whatever she did to you, you weren't looking so good there for a couple of minutes."

The bounty hunter shook his head. "I'm fine. Used a little magic to make me feel better. For now, I just want to spend time with my family and friends—especially my daughter."

A bright smile covered Alison's face. "I like the sound of that, Dad."

Forty-five minutes later, Shay stepped out of the restroom to find Lieutenant Hall standing there, her arms crossed.

The tomb raider arched an eyebrow. She'd thought they were on good terms, given what had happened during the Hansen incident and her court performance, but maybe the AET officer had discovered the truth about her and decided she couldn't look away after all.

"I don't know your complete deal," the cop began, "but I know you're a lot more than you appear to be."

Shay chuckled. "Isn't everyone in LA?" She kept her arms loose at her sides in case she needed to take the cop out.

Lieutenant Hall reached into her pocket and retrieved a small piece of paper. She held it out. "A little information that just came my way. Obviously, that crazy Drow bitch was one piece of the Oriceran side of this shit, but you saw her in court. She couldn't have done half that shit without help from our government, and I thought you might like to know who, and for that matter, which local Oricerans know our system better than Queen Haughty Bitch."

"What are you saying?"

"I don't have proof, but from what I hear, the consul and his buddy were partially behind blocking the adoption.'

Shay frowned. "But they stopped the Drow. Why would they help her and then stop her?"

The cop shrugged. "Not going to claim I get Oriceran politics." She shook her hand with the paper. "Anyway, you can't go after a consul, but there might be someone else you could go after."

The tomb raider grabbed the piece of paper and looked at it. There were two words scribbled on the paper: Senator Aaron.

Huh. So they were able to pull off what Peyton is still working on. I'll have to bust his balls about that later.

Her gaze turned flinty. This was the man who had threatened their happiness, all to help some twisted Oriceran bitch.

No. Some things weren't easy to forgive.

Shay looked up from the paper. "And what am I supposed to do with this information? You do realize I'm not gonna use it to write a sternly-worded letter?"

Lieutenant Hall shrugged. "Do whatever you want, but if it were me, I'd have a little discussion, maybe at night, to make it clear that joining up with crazy Oriceran queens isn't in the senator's best interests. Just hypothetically."

"And you think I can pull something off like that?"

"I think anyone who hangs out around James Brownstone is dangerous, let alone his girlfriend." The cop looked over her shoulder and leaned in. "Just to be clear, I'm giving this to you as part of my apology to Brownstone. Don't make me regret it. Don't kill anyone, just make them afraid."

Shay chuckled darkly. "I think I can manage that."

Tyler leaned against the wall, his arms crossed as he surveyed the bar. There were so many happy people drinking. Even some complete pieces of shit were going over to congratulate Brownstone. It turns out that not understanding women wasn't the only thing Brownstone and criminals had in common. A lot of the men were also fathers. Shitty fathers, but still fathers.

"He's a fucking dad now," the information broker mumbled. "And I keep helping him out. Maybe it's pointless to pretend that we aren't friends."

Maria came up behind him and gave him a light hug. "What was that about dads?"

"Just was thinking about how when I look at Brownstone as a dad, it's hard to hate his ass, but then again, should it make a difference?"

"Oh? Why do you say that?"

"Just saying I'm not a dad."

Maria grinned. "Who says you might be?" She smirked and pulled away from him with a wink.

Before Tyler's brain could restart, the woman disappeared into the thick crowd, heading toward Brownstone's table.

He swallowed and slapped his cheeks. She had to be fucking with him. There was no way. They'd taken precautions.

Shit. How do I get the info I really need now?

A week later, Shay crept along the roof across from her target building, her ski mask stopping the night's chill from reaching her face. Heavy clouds covered the sky, but plenty of light from the street and buildings bounced around DC, pushing true darkness away.

She snickered.

I'm probably doing one of the least-criminal things in this town tonight.

Security drones were dense in the skies of the capital, which complicated matters. If she killed the drones using a jammer or EMP, security and police would swarm the area, thinking a terrorist had arrived. Fortunately, she had a solution thanks to her friendly neighborhood hacker Peyton.

"How long do I have?" Shay whispered, knowing her throat mic would pick up more than enough for him to hear.

"Five more minutes to get inside," he responded through the receiver in her ear. "That's as long as I can spoof them without their systems recognizing what's going on. They might not immediately do anything, but I wouldn't bet on it, and if they get really squirrelly, they might send the cops. You sure about this?"

"Damned sure. There's no fucking way I'm not getting into that building tonight."

Shay sighed as she judged the distance. "Too damned far for parkour. Guess not every skill works in every situation." She reached into her backpack and pulled out a grappling gun. "And you're sure about the external alarms? I don't want to be trying to avoid gunfire when I'm hanging off the side of a building."

"Yep. At least another ten minutes on those, but I'm not crazy about this whole reactivating-everything-afterward thing. You'll end up trapped in there if something goes wrong."

The tomb raider moved to a darker corner of the roof and aimed the grappling gun, squinting. "It's fine. I've got my way out."

Peyton sighed. "And from what you described, it's not all that reliable."

Shay snickered. "You let me worry about that. I've been in tighter situations than this. Shit, I'm not even under water.

"I know, but—"

"Don't have time to debate this. It's go-time."

Shay eyed a nice ledge right outside her target window and fired. The grappling hook shot out with a hiss and clanged as it caught on the ledge. She tugged the line a few times and then leapt off the roof.

The tomb raider sailed through the air several stories

up until her boots hit the side of the other building. She grasped the gun and hit the retract button, the motor whirring as the line retracted. A moment later she arrived at her floor and a darkened window.

Too easy, as long as you have a hacker blocking the security system of a major government building hardened against terrorism, the same hacker spoofing drone feeds in a huge area, an expensive custom grappling gun, you've spent several days scouting the location, and you're willing to jump off a building in the middle of the night. Yeah, too easy.

Shay took a few deep breaths when a stiff gust hit her. If she slipped, it'd be several stories down to hard asphalt. She slipped the gun back into her backpack and pulled out a short feather. Sometimes tomb raids yielded an artifact or two that made life much easier when you needed to break into a random building.

Shay placed the feather against the window and took several deep breaths. The feather glowed, and her hand passed through glass that rippled out like the surface of water. She climbed through the magically liquified window into the darkened office.

The feather caught fire and burned into ashes, and she hissed as smoke rose to the ceiling.

Fuck. Didn't plan on that. Peyton didn't shut off the fire alarm.

Several tense seconds passed, and the smoke alarm didn't activate. Shay let out a sigh of relief.

She moved into the corner of the room and pulled out her 9mm.

Just hope the senator didn't decide to not check his messages.

Otherwise, this is gonna be a boring night for no good reason. Can't wait to meet the asshole.

She smirked. A gun-toting stranger in dark clothes and a ski mask in the corner would be a shock to anyone.

The tomb raider stood there in the darkness for five minutes until the magnetic lock on the door clicked. She grinned and hovered her finger over the short-range jammer on her right wrist. The door opened, the senator stepped inside, and he flipped the lights on.

Shay activated the jammer. The security systems would undoubtedly recognize something was going on, and security would be on their way in minutes, but it didn't matter. She'd be done with her business long before they arrived.

She lifted the gun, its outline visible in the shadows.

The senator winced. "Shit."

"I'm glad to see you read your email, Senator Aaron. It makes this far less annoying for me."

The senator narrowed his eyes, trying to peer into the darkness and make her out. "It was a fake message? A lure? Shit. Brownstone?"

The man backed up and collided with his desk, fear spreading over his face.

Shay let out a low laugh. "Not Brownstone. He wouldn't have been so fucking subtle."

"Who the hell are you, then? Why are you here?"

She waved the gun. "Now, I'm not Brownstone, but I *am* here because of him, and because you decided to help those Oricerans fuck him over. Anyway, he's busy and doesn't need to deal with you, and this situation requires finesse, not raw power."

The senator swallowed. "You're here to kill me?"

Shay snorted. "I could have killed you anytime I wanted. I could have done it from miles away. You see, the way to think about it is that if Brownstone is thunder, then I'm lightning. You can't find me. You can't stop me, but I can strike you down wherever and whenever I want."

"Then why haven't you?"

"Because it's not worth the trouble…yet." She pointed the gun at the senator's crotch, and he flinched. "But this is a warning. You're not the only one with Oriceran friends. Fuck with Brownstone again, and you'll pay. You can try to find me, but I doubt you have a lot of pull on Oriceran."

The senator shook his head. "What the fuck are you talking about?"

"You've lost, but if you try again, the gloves will come off."

Shay pulled a small opal out of her pocket. She rubbed the gem and took a deep breath.

A portal winked into existence behind her. She holstered her gun and jumped into it.

The opal burned in her hand. She arrived in a simple wooden room with no furniture, the gem in her hand reduced to powder.

A few seconds later, another portal opened. James exited, followed by Dannec.

Shay would have preferred to use her own magic guy, the gnome Tubal-Cain, but both Lieutenant Hall and Tyler were willing to vouch for Dannec. As a bonus, the Light Elf hated Drow so much that he was willing to sell James and Shay the portal stones at a considerable discount.

James wore a scabbard containing Shay's enchanted

Masamune *tachi*. She'd insisted he use the sword since she doubted their target would go down after a few bullets.

Shay yanked off her ski mask and wrapped her arms around James' neck. She gave him a deep kiss, then pulled away.

"I'll look after Alison. Just come back to us."

James gave her a lopsided grin. "I will. I promise."

Dannec cleared his throat and nodded. Another portal opened. "Let's get going."

Shay stepped through the portal and arrived in an apartment in Elf Town in LA.

She took a few deep breaths. They knew the threats on Earth and Oriceran. She'd neutralized the first one, and now it was up to James to neutralize the second.

James marched toward the bridge of dark metal that stretched across the massive cavern. He couldn't even make out the ground below and wondered how far up they were, given that there were clouds below the bridge. The sprawling Drow palace occupied the barren plateau on the other side of the bridge.

He looked at the sky. Unlike the sad washed-out sky of LA, thousands of stars filled this one.

Two Drow in armor stood at the front of the bridge, both eyeing James with a combination of confusion and suspicion.

The amulet whispered in his mind. *Begin battle. Stronger.*

The bounty hunter had bonded with the amulet before taking the portal to Oriceran. He couldn't risk any surprises since he knew how powerful the Drow could be. Without his amulet, he wouldn't last ten seconds against them.

Kill, the amulet whispered.

No, asshole. I'm not gonna take on the entire fucking Drow race. This is just about that bitch. She's got to pay for what she did.

She sent people to kill me more than a few times. It'd be unfair to the Harriken if I didn't go pay her a visit, now, wouldn't it?

Worthy enemy.

James grunted. He agreed with his little bloodthirsty chest pal. At least the queen would really give him a work-out.

He approached the guards and grinned. "What, don't get a lot of tourists from LA showing up at the palace with swords? This shit's on all the big tourist websites."

The two elves exchanged looks, and a faint glow appeared around their heads for a moment.

"Who are you?" one demanded. "State your name and business here, human."

It sounded like English to James, but he wasn't sure if they spoke the language or were using some sort of translation spell.

He patted his scabbard. "James Brownstone. I've got an appointment with Queen Laena. Trust me, she'll want to see me."

The Drow's face scrunched in confusion. He lifted his hand, and a shadow ripped from the ground and formed into a vaguely birdlike shape. The bird shot away like a bullet toward the palace. About a minute later, another shadow bird arrived from that direction and landed in the elf's hand.

Surprise spread over his face. "We're to escort you to the palace, Brownstone."

"Good. I was hoping she'd say that."

Laena, along with a dozen Drow, awaited James as he exited the bridge onto a smooth obsidian path lined with softly-glowing crystal obelisks leading directly to the palace.

Nice place. I was expecting pikes with heads and skulls in cages.

The Drow queen nodded to the two bridge guards, and they spun and started walking back to the other side of the bridge.

"Brownstone," Laena snarled, and spat on the ground. "Stubborn, brave, and stupid. You are responsible for all my problems. I'd convinced myself that I should leave you be, but then I was foolishly convinced to work within your pathetic human system. The Light Elf fools were worried about war. I should give them war for wasting my time."

James narrowed his eyes. Shay had told him what Lieutenant Hall had said, but he hadn't been sure if other Oricerans had been involved until now. The queen's threats of war now explained the Light Elves' actions. It didn't make him any happier, but he didn't plan to raid the consulate anytime soon.

Laena sneered. "Tell me why you're here. Consider your answer carefully, because if it is poorly formed, you will die in the next minute. Your arrogance in presenting yourself to me here has almost sealed your doom, insect."

James shrugged. "I just don't like you. You keep trying to kill me, and you keep fucking with my daughter."

"She is *not* your daughter," Laena screeched. "She is a Drow."

The bounty hunter shook his head. "You know, if I really thought you gave a shit this might be different, but I think this isn't even about her, and we both know it."

"Oh? What's it about then, human?"

James tapped his head. "The fucking wish. But screw you. That's for her, not for you, and not for anyone else. You can't have it."

Laena laughed. "I'm going to enjoy killing you. I'd love to take the time to flay you slowly and make you beg me to end it quickly, but I'll be satisfied just watching the life go out of your eyes. Sometimes, it's the simplest pleasures. I'm sure even your primitive human brain can understand that."

The amulet's eagerness flooded James' mind.

Kill. Become stronger. Worthy enemy.

Okay, Whispy Doom. Let's see how good you really are. If you haven't adapted as much as I hope, we're gonna get shredded here very soon.

James unsheathed his blade. "My primitive human brain understands that I need to beat your ass down."

The Drow around the queen all summoned shields and shadow blades.

Laena raised a hand and shook her head. "I will face this human alone. The rest of you will not intervene."

James pointed the sword at her. "If you swear to me that you'll leave Alison alone, I'll leave right now. Otherwise, I'm gonna end you."

"'End me?' How absurd." Laena spread her arms out. Her eyes turned solid black, and a shimmering dark nimbus surrounded her body. "You stand no chance against me. I am the queen of the Drow. I am power."

"I'd sooner stab myself than listen to you tell me this shit for a long time."

Laena stared at him with hate in her eyes. "When I kill you, James Brownstone, I'm going to cut off your head, and send it to be paraded around your precious Los Angeles as a warning to any who'd threaten the Drow. I'm tired of hiding. Tired of pretending I should care what your pathetic species thinks or feels. I will make Los Angeles bend the knee to their new queen."

James grunted. "Shut the fuck up and fight, you delusional bitch." He raised the sword and jogged toward her.

The queen smirked and raised her palm. A black orb blasted out and slammed into James. He hissed at the burn, but other than a light abrasion, the magic didn't accomplish much.

Laena blinked. "It's not possible."

Satisfaction spread from the amulet.

Guess letting those Drow blast the fuck out of us last time was worth something after all. All I need to do now is let every Oriceran race all but kill me, and then I'll be great.

The Drow queen pelted James with more blasts. The attacks shredded his shirt and stung, but he didn't take any serious wounds.

James smirked and slowed his pace. "And you're the queen? Give me a fucking break. I thought this was gonna be a real fight. It looks like it's gonna end up real one-sided."

Laena glared at him. She lifted her arm, and a shadow spear appeared in her hand. She pulled her arm back and threw the spear.

James jumped to the side to avoid the spear, but it

circled around and slammed into his shoulder before disappearing in a cloud of dark particles. He hissed at the pain spiking through his body and fell to one knee.

Fuck, that hurt.

New attack, the amulet whispered.

Yeah. Kind of figured that one out. Whatever doesn't kill you, right?

Adapt or die.

James took a deep breath and stood. "Missed my heart."

Laena's smile returned. She summoned another spear and threw it at James. This time he didn't dodge, and the spear only stung.

Whispy Doom, I think you're getting better and quicker at this shit.

James sheathed his sword. The Drow queen wasn't the only one who wanted to enjoy kicking the ass of a hated enemy. He charged toward the woman. A few punches and kicks to punish her for her bullshit were in order.

The ground exploded all around him, jagged shards of glowing obsidian tearing at his flesh. Ignoring the pain, he pushed through. Another blast annoyed him, but it didn't do much more than sting this time.

The rapture of the bloodthirsty amulet sang in his mind. *Kill. Stronger. Kill. Stronger. Adapt or die.*

Laena screamed. "I am the queen of the Drow, and you are nothing, James Brownstone. You will burn." She snapped her hands up, and a huge purple fireball roared toward James.

He threw himself to the side but hissed in pain as the explosion singed his arm and side.

Another fireball exploded in front of him and knocked

him backward. A few minor burns covered his chest. A third fireball accomplished little other than destroying his shirt.

James forced himself to stand. His entire side hurt now, but he wasn't bleeding much. He had one healing potion in his pants pocket, but he wanted to save it until he needed it. There was no way in hell he'd use Alison's wish to save his life, which meant the potion was the backup plan.

"That all you got, Laena?" The bounty hunter stumbled forward and regained his footing. "This is the terrible power of the Drow?"

A shadowy crescent shot toward him and slammed into his chest. He stumbled for a moment, grunting more from the pain of his existing wounds than the mild sting of the crescent blade.

James shook his head and continued toward the queen. "All I ever wanted was to be left alone. All Alison ever wanted was a loving family." He pointed at Laena. "The fucking Harriken got greedy and took her mother, and now you're greedy, and you want to take her father. Fuck you. You don't win today. You didn't win in court, and you won't win here."

"*You are not her father*," Laena shouted. "You're nothing." She lifted her arms to the sky again, an eerie purple glow suffusing the area around her.

The nearby Drow all ran from her.

"I'm the queen of the Drow, and you are just a human with a few trinkets. You are nothing but a worm before me."

If James didn't know better, he would have thought the amulet snorted in his mind.

Kill. Become stronger.

Don't worry, Whispy Doom. I'm gonna give her a beatdown so hard they'll be singing operas about it on Oriceran for centuries.

James charged Laena and pulled back his fist. The woman didn't move. The purple light grew in intensity. Closer. Closer.

Twenty feet…ten…five…three.

The bounty hunter grinned. It was time to end this. He threw his fist right at her face.

A bright flash followed and hurled him back. He slammed into the hard obsidian path and rolled several feet, his side and shoulder aching.

Using one hand, the bounty hunter pushed himself up and then stood.

"Okay, so not gonna end this with one punch. Fair enough." James unsheathed the blade. "How about a magic sword, then?"

He sucked in a few breaths, trying to block out the pain.

Kill. Become stronger.

I'm working on it.

The queen's form shuddered for a moment, and another blast of light forced him to look away. When he looked back the queen was gone, replaced by an undulating mass of shadowy arms outlined in a violet glow.

"DO YOU UNDERSTAND YET, BROWNSTONE?" The sound came as a chorus of reverberating voices from the arms.

"What the fuck am I supposed to understand? That you're ugly as fuck now?"

James took a deep breath. Everything had a weak spot. He just needed to find it.

"ON YOUR PLANET, YOU ARE A GOD. HERE YOU ARE AN INSECT."

"Maybe I'm a roach. They are fucking hard to kill."

The bounty hunter let out a loud bellow and charged. He slashed toward the shadow mass with the sword and the light flashed again, but this time it didn't knock him back.

A chorus of shrieks sounded as one of the shadow arms ripped off and fluttered into the sky like black dust. Several of the other arms shot out at him, their tips sharpening.

James grunted with each hit and growled as one slammed his wounded side, but they were scratching him or only giving him minor cuts.

The amulet's drunken joy at being in battle almost distracted him.

Get it in check, Whispy.

Another few slashes separated more shadow arms, but two grabbed him and flung him away. He landed hard with a grunt. A second later, violet lightning blasted from several of the arms and slammed into him.

James cried out as he sailed backward, pain spreading from both his side and chest. Another series of lightning blasts shot into him, and he hissed as they deepened the ache in his previous wounds.

Using the sword to brace himself, the bounty hunter forced himself back to his feet.

Come on, Whispy. Does she have a heart or something? Help me out. We're not gonna win a battle of attrition.

Agony blasted into his eyes, and he squeezed them shut.

Laena's combined voices cackled into the darkness.

"BEG NOW, BROWNSTONE, AND YOUR DEATH WILL BE QUICK. OTHERWISE, I WILL PULL YOU APART PIECE BY PIECE."

Open, partner. Open. See.

James forced his eyes open. Through the pain, he could see it now—buried within one of the arms, a beating heart.

"AFTER YOU DIE, I WILL GO AND TAKE THE GIRL. I WILL PUNISH HER FOR HER INSOLENCE. SHE WILL GIVE HER WISH TO ME AND SUFFER FOR TURNING HER BACK ON THE DROW. IF SHE WISHES TO BE A HUMAN, THEN SHE IS DISPOSABLE LIKE ONE."

Cleansing rage washed away the pain. James roared and sprinted right toward the heart, his sword pointed forward.

"I will fucking destroy you, bitch," the bounty hunter bellowed.

Blast after blast shot debris around him or struck him, but the pain didn't reach his brain. He kept running, ignoring everything but his target.

James' sword pierced the arm and went into the heart.

The deep screams echoed over the entire plateau. A wave of force slammed into James and knocked him back a good ten yards. The *tachi* clattered out of his hand, sliding off the obsidian path onto the packed, smooth pebbles beside it.

Stronger, the amulet whispered.

James sat up. Laena lay on the ground, back in her humanoid form, bleeding from her mouth, but still breathing. Several cuts covered her body, but shadows were seeping into them, and the injuries were already closing.

Fuck. Maybe the head, not the heart?

James squeezed the bridge of his nose, the pain throbbing all over his body now, including his head.

The bounty hunter reached into his pocket, grateful that the potion was still there. His shirt was nothing but a collar at this point, and his pants had more holes than Swiss cheese. The scabbard was a burned mess, and he hoped Shay wouldn't be too pissed since the sword was still fine.

He downed the potion and waited. Fifteen seconds later, he was a new man in need of an equally new outfit.

James stood and grabbed the sword. He marched over toward the queen, but a dozen Drow moved toward her.

Shit. Even with you, Whispy, I don't know if I can take them.

Fight. Become stronger.

"I've got no beef with you," James shouted. "My only beef is with her."

The Drow ignored him and marched toward the queen. They surrounded her, spacing themselves out equidistantly. They raised their hands and chanted something in a hissing, sibilant language James didn't understand.

Laena shook her head, sitting up. "No. You can't do this. *No!*"

Dark purple lines of energy formed around the queen, trapping her in a cage of light. She screamed as tendrils of light shot into her. She twitched and thrashed inside the cage, her smooth skin wrinkling. After a minute of unearthly keening, the regal and beautiful woman from before was replaced by a withered crone whimpering inside the energy cage.

James made his way over and shook his head. "What the fuck just happened?"

One of the twelve Drow stepped out of line. James recognized him as one of the guards from the courthouse.

The Drow nodded toward the queen. "Most of her power has been taken, and because of that, the magic she used to resist time has taken its toll. If she were on Earth, with its still-limited magic, she would likely wither away into dust."

"I don't get it. Is this some sort of coup shit?" James pointed with the sword at the queen.

"Of a sort. It is a new era, a new time. No one on Oriceran can survive by mindlessly doing what they did before." The Drow shook his head. "You had already defeated her most powerful supporters, but none of us were brave enough to face her. Tonight you gave us our opportunity. It's time for a new age of the Drow."

James nodded. "Like I said, I've got no beef with you."

"About the girl…"

The bounty hunter brought up his sword. "I'm still her dad."

The Drow raised a placating hand. "We don't wish to earn your wrath, James Brownstone. We simply wonder if she could visit on occasion."

James lowered the sword. He pursed his lips and nodded. "When she's ready. It *is* her mother's heritage, after all, but not without me at her side."

"Of course. We understand now, all too well, how far

you're willing to go to protect the girl." He nodded toward the queen. "If you wish, we will allow you to finish her."

He stared at the now-unconscious former queen and shook his head. "Fuck her. I want her to suffer for a while. Death's too quick for her after all the bullshit she pulled."

The corners of the Drow's mouth turned up in a slight smile. "You're more like us than you realize, James Brownstone."

"I might be a loving father, but I'm not a good man."

James reached into his pocket to pull out his portal stone. It was gone, thanks to the hole burned into his pocket.

"Son of a bitch. Hey, one last favor to ask. I need a ride home."

Multiple grills filled the park. Sergeant Mack and the men of Camp Brownstone worked on preparing food: barbeque, hot dogs, and burgers. A meat lover's paradise.

Tables decorated with colorful cloths surrounded the cooking area, neighborhood locals at some, cops at others. Father McCartney sat with Charlyce and the kids from the orphanage at yet another.

James smiled as he surveyed the area. It was a nice environment for his men to practice their cooking skills. His smile faded as he eyed the charred wreck on his plate.

"How the fuck do you burn a hot dog, Trey? If you can't handle hot dogs, barbeque's gonna destroy you."

Sergeant Mack laughed from a nearby grill and shook his head.

Trey shrugged. "This shit ain't like dropping a bounty, big man. You've got to deal with heat."

Lachlan hissed when he burned himself trying to turn a

burger. "Fuck. We need to be all strategic and shit with this. Tricky-ass flames. I think I prefer a microwave."

"Wonder what Sun Tzu has to say about barbeque," Shorty mused aloud.

Royce wandered over and laughed. "The closest thing I can think of is, 'When the men do not hang their cooking-pots over the campfires, showing that they will not return to their tents, you may know that they are determined to fight to the death.'"

Trey furrowed his brow. "So a motherfucker who doesn't get the wood in his pit burning is ready to fight to the death?"

James grunted. "They deserve to die anyway for disrespecting the barbeque."

Everyone laughed.

Alison and Shay wandered over from Father McCartney's table.

"What's so funny?" the teen asked.

"Barbeque," Trey explained.

Alison and Shay both groaned.

A couple of hours later Alison was on her way back home from the park, a smile on her face. She loved the School of Necessary Magic, but being with James and Shay had reminded her what it was truly like to be loved and cherished by a mother and father, even if Shay wanted to keep insisting she was nothing more than her aunt.

Just wait and see. I'm sure Dad will make a move sooner rather than later.

Alison grinned at the thought.

"Aren't we a sweet young thing?" came a voice from behind her.

The teen spun, frowning. She shuddered at the lust and general vileness in the energy of the man behind her.

"Excuse me. I was on my way home."

The man shook his head. "Ain't no one around, girl. Maybe you should keep me company. Or you can give me anything you have on you, and I'll walk away. Nice necklace. Pretty sweet deal, don't you think?"

Alison took a deep breath. She didn't need the Aegis Pendant for an idiot like this.

Okay, how would Dad or Aunt Shay want me to handle this?

The girl painted her face with an arrogant smirk. Confidence was key in the early part of a battle.

"Walk away, dirtbag, and you won't get hurt."

The man snorted. "You keep running that mouth, little girl, and this is gonna hurt a lot more than it needs to. Now give me the fucking necklace and anything else you got on you."

Alison shook her head. There were so many things she could do to him, but for some reason, she wanted it to be a little more visceral and a little more painful. If she were too subtle, he wouldn't learn his lesson.

There was a sudden *snick*, and she could see the energy of a knife.

The man pointed into the distance. "We're gonna walk between those two houses, and you're gonna keep your mouth fucking shut if you know what's good for you. Last chance, bitch."

Alison lifted her hand. "It's actually *your* last chance to walk away."

"I've had enough—"

He screamed as her summoned flames burned the hand with the knife. He dropped the weapon and clutched his hand. "What the fuck?"

Alison shook her head. "I gave you a lot of warnings. You don't really have anyone to blame but yourself."

The man sprinted away, whimpering.

Alison's heart rate kicked up as someone shouted from behind her and she spun, lifting her hands.

Two men were rushing toward her, but she relaxed after a moment. The souls were familiar, as were their voices. Shorty and Max.

All the men now knew her secrets, which annoyed and comforted her at the same time because they'd become more protective of her.

Shorty arrived first. "Yo, Alison, you all right? We saw that bitch pull that knife, but we was way far out."

Max nodded.

Alison snorted. "Bitch, *please*. He didn't stand a chance."

Shorty and Max laughed.

She shrugged. "You don't fuck with a Drow princess, especially not Alison Brownstone."

FINIS

First, THANK YOU for not only reading this story, but also reading through the back to our *Author Notes*, too!

When I was working on the beats for this book, I had a hard time getting into the groove of a story. *Any* story for this book.

The problem, I finally figured out, was I didn't know who the bad guys were. Normally, James is fighting someone physically and everything plays out from there. Occasionally, it is an antagonist with a bit more of a non-physical challenge, which often requires physical reactions.

#GoBigBOOM! (#aAmIRight?)

But, what to do when the story is about Alison's adoption? THAT was supposed to be the big deal of the book, and how is that much of a challenge?

Well, except the teenager part, that's always a challenge.

Then, EUREKA!

I realized that those damned Drow I thought were gone would absolutely not appreciate what was going to go on, and the government would likely try to minimize the blowback by supporting an effort to make sure Brownstone couldn't adopt Alison.

"Oh shit," I thought to myself. "That wouldn't go down well at all."

Then, it occurred to me that in court, the government would be seeking to prove their point that Brownstone is not a proper person to adopt Alison. Further, he was going to need to do some defense, but how do you defend yourself?

He wouldn't.

Nope, his friends—those he had helped—would stand up for him and prove the government was full of hot air.

Right up to the point the Drow queen would show up. Her little display would hurt Brownstone, perhaps. But it would do one thing for absolutely sure, which is make him decide it was time to take her out.

Because, die trying or not, Alison wouldn't be safe until she wasn't a problem. "Aunt" Shay would take care of the government asshole, and we get a nice family finish.

Except, Alison didn't get her time to shine.

Until the end.

"I'm Alison Brownstone, *bitch*."

Those, I think, will be the first words of her new series after she graduates from the School of Necessary Magic.

Coming 1ˢᵗ Quarter, 2019

Ad Aeternitatem,

Michael Anderle

The Unbelievable Mr. Brownstone

* Michael Anderle *

Feared by Hell (1) - Rejected by Heaven (2) - Eye For An Eye (3) - Bring the Pain (4) - She is the Widow Maker (5) - When Angels Cry (6) - Fire with Fire (7) - Hail To The King (08) - Alison Brownstone (9)

I Fear No Evil

* Martha Carr and Michael Anderle *

Kill the Willing (1) - Bury the Past, But Shoot it First (2) - Reload Faster (3) - Dead In Plain sight (4) - Tomb Raiding PHD (5)

School of Necessary Magic

* Judith Berens *

Dark Is Her Nature (1) Bright Is Her Sight (2) - Wary Is Her Love (3) - Strong Is Her Hope (4)

Rewriting Justice

* Martha Carr and Michael Anderle *

Justice Served Cold (1) - Vengeance Served Hot (2) - Bounty Hunter Inc (03)

The Leira Chronicles

* Martha Carr and Michael Anderle *

Waking Magic (1) - Release of Magic (2) - Protection of Magic (3)

- Rule of Magic (4) - Dealing in Magic (5) - Theft of Magic (6) - Enemies of Magic (7) - Guardians of Magic (8)

The Soul Stone Mage Series

* Sarah Noffke and Martha Carr *

House of Enchanted (1) - The Dark Forest (2) - Mountain of Truth (3) - Land of Terran (4) - New Egypt (5) - Lancothy (6) - Virgo (7)

The Kacy Chronicles

* A.L. Knorr and Martha Carr *

Descendant (1) - Ascendant (2) - Combatant (3) - Transcendent (4)

The Midwest Magic Chronicles

* Flint Maxwell and Martha Carr*

The Midwest Witch (1) - The Midwest Wanderer (2) - The Midwest Whisperer (3) - The Midwest War (4)

The Fairhaven Chronicles

* with S.M. Boyce *

Glow (1) - Shimmer (2) - Ember (3) - Nightfall (4)

Michael Anderle Social
Website:
http://kurtherianbooks.com/

Email List:
http://kurtherianbooks.com/email-list/

Facebook Here:
https://www.facebook.com/OriceranUniverse/
https://www.
facebook.com/TheKurtherianGambitBooks/

www.ingramcontent.com/pod-product-compliance
Lightning Source LLC
Chambersburg PA
CBHW050235110726
47898CB00007B/2160